Someone She Once Knew

by

Melissa Klein

Someone She Once Knew

Contact Information: info@thewildrosepress.com

Cover Art by *Diana Carlile*

The Wild Rose Press, Inc.
PO Box 708
Adams Basin, NY 14410-0708
Visit us at www.thewildrosepress.com

Publishing History
First Edition, 2021
Trade Paperback ISBN 978-1-5092-3653-4
Digital ISBN 978-1-5092-3654-1
Previously Published:
Someone She Once Knew, Rusty Wheels Media, 8/16/18

Published in the United States of America

The giant of a man stood in the center of the room, triaging the injured, issuing orders to her staff, taking control of the disaster's aftermath.

Julia picked her way over to him. "Did my people bring you a first aid kit?"

"Yes." He looked her way for a moment before calling to one of her staff. "I need more bandages."

A long-ago memory flashed in her mind. That voice—she'd heard it before. She cocked her head. Studied his profile. Her mind raced.

"Do I know you?"

"What? No."

Those eyes. She'd known only one person with that shade of brown. He'd disappeared from her life more than a decade ago. "Who are you?"

The man crossed his arms. "Nobody."

Not so. She felt it.

Julia studied him closer… Massive legs. Intricate tattoos running down both arms. Close-cropped hair. Piercings. His face was one that rang no bells. But the amber-hued eyes, narrowed to slits… She put a hand to her mouth to stifle the gasp. "Luke?"

He stiffened but kept treating the lady in front of him.

"My God, I can't believe it." What had happened to the handsome young man who'd been her first love? "What? How? When?" Her mouth tripped over her brain. Even if her thoughts had been clear, she couldn't put into words the question her heart had asked over and over and over the past decade. Why had he left her behind without a word of goodbye?

Praise for Someone She Once Knew

"This is a southern romance and one where the characters are true to their roots, they are both strong and the chemistry between them is hot! I like the way the author built the story, piece by piece building the story and the tension and keeping me turning those pages."

~ *LeMiliere*

Dedication

To my dear Aunt Ann.
Thank you for all your love and support.

Chapter One

Julia Wilkes swept open a set of French doors leading to Highlands' upper balcony. She led Richard Pierce, a capital investor, across silver-gray flagstones to the railing then gestured to the property she desperately needed to purchase if she was going to take her resort to the next level.

"Wolfe Winery is just beyond the ninth tee, so you can see how easily I could incorporate vineyard tours and wine tastings into Highland's amenities."

The gentleman in his early forties pushed his wire-rimmed glasses further up the bridge of his nose. "Not hard to picture, even with all this rain. However, what I want is more than a visual. I've been over your business plan. Looked at the finances. What I want is something I can't get from reading documents." He stepped closer. "I want to see your passion for this endeavor."

Passion. Pride. Possibilities. They all motivated her drive for excellence.

Julia squared her shoulders. Much rode on this presentation, so a small measure of panic also spurred her onward. "That won't be a problem. Outside my son, it's my favorite topic of conversation. I'm completely in love with Highlands, Mr. Pierce."

He touched her arm. "Please, call me Richard."

Unease danced along her spine. Theirs was a strictly business relationship, and she intended to keep it that way. “As you wish, *Richard.*” She stepped out of his reach. “With Atlanta just twenty miles to the south, I’ve been able to keep us booked with garden parties, charity events, and weddings well into the autumn. Additionally, families come here to enjoy our Sunday brunch and often stay for a stroll through our gardens. All fifty acres contain indigenous species selected by me. I believe in creating an environment that draws people closer to nature as well as each other.”

He glanced at the view—which had inspired her to purchase the neglected hotel—then turned his attention to her. “It’s as lovely as its owner.”

Her eyes widened, but she ignored the comment. “We have six miles of trails and horses for every skill level. Well-known athletes from around the south have played the par-three golf course.”

What she failed to say was the barn needed repairs, and the reason men and women from the region’s many sports teams played there was to benefit the charity events she hosted. She might be new to the business world, but she’d spent a lifetime hiding flaws. One never acknowledged anything less than perfection or inappropriate compliments; at least not in the circles in which her family traveled.

“With the purchase of the winery, Atlanta’s elite will have even more reason to seek out North Georgia’s beauty instead of traveling to Europe for their vacations or to California for a wine country tour.”

She sounded like a commercial, but now wasn’t the time for understatement. Her connections to Atlanta’s old money only went so far. If she was going to grow the business she’d spent every day for the past three years building, she needed to expand. That required money and lots of it. Far more than she had. What her family's name held in prestige and pedigree, it lacked in cash. "Our spa has every amenity a person—"

A crack of thunder drowned out the rest of her spiel and sent a shiver across her skin. "Perhaps, we should return to my office. I can have one of my staff bring us tea." What had been predicted as simply passing showers was gaining intensity.

They crossed through the gentlemen's lounge, decorated in gold, red, and greens, on their way downstairs. Rachel Sams, her second-in-command, met her by the bank of elevators. "Sorry to bother you, Ms. Wilkes," the slender woman said, playing her professional role instead of the treasured friend she also was. "The bride and her parents would like to speak with you."

Julia stopped herself mid eye-roll. Dealing with high-maintenance guests came with the territory.

"It seemed quite urgent. There was hand wringing involved." Humor made Rachel's words dance.

Julia had known branches of the bride's family since her days at Woodruff Academy, and the Alexanders were as high-strung as they were well-heeled. "I imagine they're second guessing their decision to hold the ceremony outdoors."

Rachel shrugged. "I wouldn't know. They insisted on speaking with you."

"If you'll excuse me. This needs my attention."

Richard nodded, his expression never once giving away his thoughts. "By all means. I understand the demands of business." The smooth as glass words rolled off his tongue in an accent-less voice. She'd been acquainted with the man through her mother's country club for several years. However, when she turned down her ex-husband's, offer to purchase Wolfe Winery for her, he suggested she contact Richard for the capital she needed.

"Ms. Sams will show you to the downstairs library." Her suggestion would not only make him comfortable, but it would also allow her staff to potentially observe him doing something that would indicate his mindset. "I'll join you shortly, and we can discuss particulars further."

She found the bride and her parents in the bridal suite on the hotel's third floor. Entering the room painted in neutral ivory and gray to compliment any bride's color palette, she found the family gathered at the window. Julia admired the asymmetrical gown. "Kelsey, you're breath taking. At least the early-twenties bride was until she turned to reveal a face red with tears.

Her father crossed the room in a couple strides, coming chest-to-chest with Julia. He flung an arm toward the windows. "It's raining."

Lovely smile, gentle voice, spine of steel.

The first two parts of her mantra had been drilled into her by her mother since birth—the last was her own addition. "Yes, sir, it is."

The mother-of-the-bride put an arm around her daughter. "What are you going to do about it?"

Julia bit her lip to keep the retort inside where it belonged. She'd warned the Alexanders of the perils of an outdoor wedding. "The Magnolia Ballroom is available. There will be a small price difference, but my people can have it ready in time." They were lucky she had a cancellation. Thanks to a recent article in *Atlanta*

Bride, the gardens and ballrooms were booked every weekend.

Mr. Alexander's face turned red. "This wedding is completely out of hand."

"I'll throw in an extra appetizer," she said, speaking the language of a man with a reputation for frugality.

"Those date and bacon wraps we had at the tasting?"

Did the guy think she was stupid? Those things cost a fortune to make. "Shrimp puffs." Chef kept several hundred of those in the freezer. "Your guests will love it."

Bucky Alexander threw up a hand in resignation then stormed out of the room mumbling something about pre-nups.

Ahhh. The song of her people. Money was their god, and legal documents their hymn of praise. Julia turned to the bride, intent on helping her focus on the ceremony ahead and not the details. "Don't worry about a thing." She passed her a tissue. "Rain on your wedding day is good luck, and I promise the ballroom will be perfect. Just concentrate on the honeymoon."

A small smile played at the young woman's lips. "He's taking me to Bermuda."

"Be sure to walk under the moon gate. That's also good luck." Not that it helped her own marriage. Julia eyed the young bride, seeing herself in the dewy-eyed optimism. The couple needed all the luck they could get. Given their ages, and the fact the groom didn't have two nickels to rub together, Julia gave the marriage a year.

When had she gotten so cynical? She loved

weddings. They were her favorite part of owning a resort. She still believed in marriage. Though her own had failed. Julia was finally in a good place. She and Paul were happily divorced. They made good co-parents. After some time in family counseling. Maybe she needed a weekend away at a quiet resort.

Laughing internally at her own joke, she patted the bride on the shoulder. “I’ll leave you to finish getting ready. I’m going to get my staff started on prepping the ballroom.”

****

Luke Chevalier killed the motorcycle’s engine and tugged off his helmet. Rain pelted his shorn head and ran down the collar of his jacket, but nothing could keep him from savoring the moment years in the making. He crossed the gravel drive to wait on the porch for the young woman from the local real estate agency to exit her car. In a former life, he’d have held an umbrella for her as she navigated the puddles. Instead, he stood on the far side of the porch and tried to look as benign as his large, leather-clad body would let him. Even if he’d been dressed in a suit and tie, he wouldn’t have been able to disguise what over a decade of hard living had done to him.

“As I mentioned on the phone, the property has twenty acres.” Her gaze darted between him and the lockbox. “The pasture is in rough shape, and the house needs updating, but it has four bedrooms and three full baths.” Her voice shook as she detailed the house’s features. “There’s also a small apartment over the stable.”

He pointed past the woman to the inside of the house. “I’d like to see for myself, if that’s okay.”

"Yes, of course." She scooted out of his way. "I'll give you some room to look around." She made no move to join him, likely preferring a soaking to being hemmed inside with him.

He took no offense at her behavior. Given his collection of tattoos and piercings, he half expected her to not get out of her car. "Thank you, ma'am. I'll be quick."

A crash of thunder had him glancing back at his motorcycle. Man, it was going to be a long ride back to Ohio. He'd have made a different transportation choice if there'd been another to make. He sold his truck along with everything else he owned to buy this place. It wouldn't matter the price or if he had to work another decade, he was buying his childhood home. It was his fault it had gone out of his family's hands, and it was his responsibility to get it back.

Memories flooded as he wandered through the living room on the way upstairs. The same brown carpet covered the floors, and his boyhood room was still navy blue. All that was missing were the people who turned the four walls into a home. He rubbed at the ache in the center of his chest, but self-pity was a luxury he couldn't afford. Five minutes later, he was back on the porch. "Tell the sellers I'll give them full asking price. I want to close in a week."

The realtor's mouth gaped for a moment before she could find her words. "That's not possible. You'll need to arrange for financing. Then there's the title search."

He pulled his checkbook out of his leather jacket. "I'm paying cash." He tore off the check for the earnest money he'd already written out. "Seven, days," he said, jonesing to get on the road. He had no plans to live there himself, but it would be the perfect place for his sister to raise her eleven-year-old son.

****

Worry dogged Julia's steps as she left the bridal party. The storm no longer effected the wedding. What about her horses? Her favorite, D'Artagnan, was temperamental on a good day, but the stallion hated storms as much as he did most people. However, with Richard waiting, she didn't have the time to run down to the barn to check on him or the mares. Instead, she texted her barn manager on the way to the library, instructing him to make certain her animals were secured in their stalls.

Stepping into the bookcase-lined room, she found her staff had done as she directed, serving him Highlands' signature tea. "Richard." When he sprang to his feet, she motioned for him to return to his seat as she sank into the club chair next to him. "Thank you for your patience. I hope my staff has made you comfortable."

She'd decorated the room in deep brown hues and oxblood leather to give the space an English country ambiance. The man at her side looked perfectly at home in the room. Dressed in a bespoke suit and silk tie, he could easily have been plucked from one of the Regency romances she loved to read.

He angled his body to face her head-on. "Absolutely." He offered her a cool smile. "I hope I'm going to be availing myself of your hospitality more frequently in the future."

"I'd like nothing better." Some of her tension eased.

That's a good sign, right? Right?

Every bank in Atlanta had turned her down, even the one her great-grandfather helped found. "I wondered if you had any further questions for me."

"Just one comes to mind." He tapped his mouth with the tip of his finger. "Why isn't your former husband investing? Paul spoke of your business in such glowing terms. I can't help but think he knows something you haven't revealed."

Julia's pulse spiked, and a string of epitaphs rushed to her lips. She bit them back. A lady might never swear, but that didn't mean she'd be a doormat. "I've disclosed all my financial records, both personal and business." She met his gaze. "I don't want him to invest. I can succeed without his help."

He leaned back, a smug grin creasing his face. "Such furor, I like it."

She wanted to smack that smile right off his face, but she couldn't afford to lose her last chance to make her dream a reality. She'd liquidated all her assets to buy the resort and the small amount of money her father left went to offset her mother's upkeep. For most people, the modest profit Highlands made last year would be enough. Most people didn't have Helena Ansley Chandler for a mother, a woman who once spent a hundred grand in a single shopping trip to Paris. Her childhood home also needed a major restoration if it was to survive another hundred years. Otherwise, she might have to consider selling the place.

Julia stood, tugging her jacket in place. "If you have no further questions, I have guests who need my attention." It wasn't just material needs that drove her. People had been underestimating her since childhood. Perhaps, not underestimating so much as expected her to fill a role she didn't want. She'd been one of those ladies-who-lunched. It left her empty. Two things fed her soul: her son, Aiden, and Highlands.

She turned to leave, but he stilled her with a hand to her arm. "I apologize if I offended. It was simply a question that needed to be asked. I admire your independence."

She let out a breath. "Apology accepted. If you'll excuse me, I really must see that the ballroom is ready. Please let me know if you require any more documentation."

"I'd like to stay if that's all right. Observe you and your staff in action." A crash of thunder rattled the walls. "Besides, the storm seems to be getting worse."

"Please, make yourself at home." Once again, she wished she had time to check on her four-legged babies. Thankfully, Paul had Aiden for the weekend so the six-year-old could attend the birthday party of a classmate at the Atlanta School for the Deaf.

Back in the main corridor, it didn't take but a moment to locate Rachel. "How's the Magnolia room coming?"

"All done. That was brilliant of you to start setting things up last night."

Julia brushed off the compliment. "Just watched the Weather Channel." With the wedding preparations complete, she had a moment to slip down to the barn.

"Don't forget to change your shoes before you check on the horses."

"Mind reader. I'll just grab some sugar cubes—" The roar of the storm distracted Julia from their conversation. Her eyes widened. "Is that the storm siren?"

"I think so."

Julia mentally ran through the list of outdoor furniture that needed to be secured. "Pull up the weather app on your phone. How long is this supposed to last?"

"There's a severe thunderstorm warning for the next hour."

Welcome to Georgia in spring, where the weather was as temperamental as an aging debutante. "If rain is good luck for a wedding, wonder what a thunderstorm is?"

****

Luke made a left at the end of the gravel road, taking him toward the interstate. Every moment he spent in Magnolia Valley increased the ache in his chest. As he gunned the engine and kicked up gravel, the rain got busy making things harder. By the time he made it another mile, driving through the storm was no longer an option.

He chanced a glance at the approaching storm behind him. A bank of greenish-yellow clouds had him tossing aside plans to ride out the weather under an overpass. His bike was fast, but not as fast as the freight train bearing down on him. The sign up ahead gave him the first ray of hope.

Highlands Resort it was.

Racing up the tree-lined drive, hail began pelting his back. As a gust of wind kicked the bike sideways, he tightened his grip on the handlebars and aimed for the covered entrance. He came in for a screaming landing, cut the engine, and dismounted in a fluid move. God, he hated leaving his bike, but he doubted the folks who ran the resort would appreciate him riding it into the lobby.

Luke took one last look behind him in time to see his bike topple onto its side. The distinctive churning of wind and the telltale freight-train roar added fuel to his feet. His legs ate up the marble lobby on his way to finding shelter.

He turned a corner putting some wall between him and the tornado just as the glass wall of the lobby shattered. To his right a set of double doors blew open, letting out the frantic shouts of party guests.

A woman bolted out of a smaller door, smacking squarely into him. "My God, the horses." She tried to sidestep him.

Luke loved horses better than he did most people, but he wasn't about to let anyone into that mess. "Hold up, lady." He grasped her by the shoulders. "That's not a storm, it's a tornado." The sound of twisting wood punctuated his comment.

"You don't understand." She struggled against him.

He did, but that changed nothing. The interior walls began to quake, putting a halt to any argument. The woman froze for a moment before springing into action. "In here." She pulled him into a large ballroom filled with wedding guests. He'd have preferred a small broom closet to the openness, but it beat the hell out of the hallway he could hear getting battered on the other side.

Luke kept an eye on the woman's retreating form, a twinge of familiarity tickling the back of his mind. He should have backed away, blended into the crowd, or as much as a six-foot-six-inch man with an ear gauge and pierced brow could blend into an upscale party.

The woman turned back to him, tilting her face to directly meet his gaze. "We need to take cover under one of the tables."

My God. Her words were a jumble as he took in a face etched in his memories. Of all the people he most wanted to avoid, Julia Chandler ranked top of the list. He waited for her to recognize him, or worse, pull back in fear as people often did.

There was no time for reaction. The wall at her back groaned, bowed, and then exploded. Luke watched as shards of drywall and lumber sprayed the room for an instant before everything turned to black.

Chapter Two

Luke came to with a weight pressing against his chest. He sucked in a breath of dust-filled air and pushed against a section of wall. As he did, he looked up to see a light fixture the size of a small car swinging precariously over his head. With a great shove, he pushed the wood and sheetrock off and rolled out of the way as the chandelier let out a great moan and crashed to the floor. His pulse thrumming in his ears, he clambered to his feet and looked for a pathway out of the room. A rain-scented breeze rushed in from the gaping hole that was once the hotel's front doors. All that separated him from escape was a few debris-filled feet.

Instead of taking the sensible route, he turned his back on a chance to leave undetected and began digging through the rubble for the woman he'd left behind more than a decade ago.

"Julia." Dust filled his lungs and cut off his words. He sank to the floor, pushing aside bits of drywall, wedding decorations, and collapsed chairs. Every self-preservationist instinct screamed for him to run, even as he dug through the rubble. He uncovered a body and held his breath as he turned the person over.

"I'm good." A man moaned, sounding anything but fine. "Help me find my wife."

The pair combed through the layers of smashed

furniture and ceiling tiles until they uncovered a woman dressed in a yellow suit. Luke took a moment to see her injuries weren't life-threatening then turned in the direction where he'd last seen Julia. With each second that passed, desperation sunk its claws a little deeper.

Off to his right, he caught a flash of light-blonde hair. He waded toward the woman just as a tall, slender man dressed in what was a nice suit pulled her to her feet and entwined her in his arms.

Luke froze.

Pain as sharp and fresh as if it were new instead of years old pierced his chest. How could he have ever thought she still needed him?

Go! Leave before she sees you.

A guest tugged on his arm. "Help me with this table." A man in a tuxedo pulled him farther into the destroyed ballroom. "The wedding party is trapped."

Luke methodically moved around the room, pulling people from underneath the rubble. All the while, his ears strained for the sound of sirens. Hearing only cries of the injured, he turned to a passing waiter. "Get me a first aid kit. I need towels. Anything else you can find to use as bandages." He hadn't used his medical degree since leaving the University of Georgia's school of Veterinary Medicine, and little of that focused on human anatomy. Blood was blood, broken bones were broken bones, and when shit went down, even long-ago training kicked in.

****

"I'm fine." Julia pushed out of Richard's embrace. "Let me go." She drew in a deep breath and immediately wished she hadn't as she choked on the dust filling the air. She retched so hard tears came to her eyes. “I have guests to see to.”

He let his arms fall to his side. “But of course.”

Giving little notice to the offended look on his face, she turned to the center of the ballroom. She gasped, unable to comprehend the destruction. “My God.”

The south wall of the ballroom had collapsed. Most of the tables had been overturned, save the one holding the wedding cake. One of the wall sconces had plunged through the center of the multi-tiered confection, smashing the porcelain bride and groom.

Her gaze darted to the head table where the wedding party had been seated before the tornado struck. The groom pulled his new wife to her feet. “Thank goodness.”

Creaking drew her attention to the ceiling. One of the magnificent chandeliers she’d purchased from an estate sale already lay in a twisted heap, and its twin danced on the end of an electrical wire. Her heart seized. “Look out! Get out of the way.” Seconds later, it crashed to the floor.

Moans and cries for help followed. How many of her guests were injured? She pulled her phone from her pocket but found she didn’t have a signal. “Someone call nine-one-one.”

“I just got off from them.” Richard came alongside her. “The dispatcher told me they were sending rescuers our way, but the tornado came through your downtown before it got to us.”

Magnolia Valley had only a volunteer fire department, so they could be on their own for some time even if the roads were passable. “Is anyone here a medical professional?”

"I think that guy is." Her head waiter, Jose, pointed to the stranger who'd prevented her from leaving the building—and probably saved her life.

He'd stripped out of his leather jacket and was holding his shirt to someone's arm. "Find out what he needs and get it to him." Julia gingerly crossed the debris to what was once the front door of her hotel. Several oaks blocked the drive, but it appeared rescue units would be able to wind their way around them. In the distance sirens wailed. She returned to the ballroom to let her guests know help was on the way.

Back in the destroyed room full of injured, one man caught her attention—and not simply because of his size. The giant of a man stood in the center of the room, triaging the injured, issuing orders to her staff, taking control of the disaster's aftermath.

Julia picked her way over to him. "Did my people bring you a first aid kit?"

"Yes." He looked her way for a moment before calling to one of her staff. "I need more bandages and find some place for the uninjured to wait."

A long-ago memory flashed in her mind. That voice—she'd heard it before. She cocked her head. Studied his profile. Her mind raced. He ignored her, finishing bandaging a cut on a guest's forehead.

"Do I know you?"

"What? No."

Those eyes. She'd known only one person with that shade of brown. He'd disappeared from her life more than a decade ago. "*Who* are you?"

The man crossed his arms. "Nobody."

Not so. She felt it.

He moved on to another injured person.

Julia studied him closer... Massive legs. Intricate tattoos running down both arms. Close-cropped hair. Piercings. His face was one that rang no bells. But the amber-hued eyes, narrowed to slits… She put a hand to her mouth to stifle the gasp. “Luke?”

He stiffened but kept treating the lady in front of him.

“My God, I can’t believe it.” What had happened to the handsome young man who’d been her first love? “What? How? When?” She stammered, her mouth tripping over her brain. Even if her thoughts had been clear, she couldn’t put into words the question her heart had asked over and over and over the past decade. Why had he left her behind without a word of goodbye?

“Luke, it’s you.” She touched his arm.

“People need my help.” He turned his back on her.

“Please.” She took his enormous hand in hers. “I want to talk to you.”

“Listen, lady,” he barked. “I’m busy here. Now, do you have someplace the uninjured can wait or not?”

Julia released his hand. “I don’t know.” His lack of reaction to seeing her again stung. “I haven’t seen the extent of the damage, but I’ll check.” She couldn’t believe it was him after all these years. Save the eyes, everything about him had changed, especially his demeanor.

“Sooner rather than later.” He bit out the words before stalking off toward another call for help.

Luke retreated, engulfed in the tangle of people and debris. He took a knee, leaning over one of the wedding guests. What had become of the young man with so much promise whom she’d given her heart to?

Julia tucked away her myriad of questions. She had

more pressing matters... Later, much later given the disaster surrounding her, she'd track Luke down. For now, her guests needed her.

"Libby," she called to one of her employees. "Bring out all the bottled water we have."

"Will do, Ms. Wilkes."

Julia followed Libby out of the room in search of an undamaged place where her guests could rest while they waited for the roads to be cleared. With each step she took and every room she surveyed, her despair grew. In the space of seconds, she'd gone from stepping over the great divide of financial success to square one. Not even square one. When she'd purchased Highlands it had needed repairs, but nothing like this.

After surveying some of the damage, she returned to the Magnolia Room. She brushed her hand over her dress, dusting off some of the drywall bits then smoothed a hand over her hair. "Ladies and gentlemen, if I could have your attention for a moment." Though all eyes were on her as she began her announcement, only Luke's mattered.

"Please join me in the lobby where my staff and I will direct you to our unoccupied rooms. You'll be able to clean up and rest until the roads are passable. I also will have food and beverages in the Nineteenth Hole shortly."

A battered and shaken Rachel met her in the lobby. Tears filled the stoic woman's eyes, setting Julia's pulse into triple digits. "We weren't the only ones hit. The storm cut a path through downtown Atlanta."

In that moment, the ruin around her ceased to matter. "What happened? What do you know?"

Rachel dashed tears from her eyes. "When you

didn't respond to his text, Paul sent me a message. He and Aiden were at his mother's house when it hit. They made it into the basement just in time."

"Thank God." After a quick hug, the two got busy passing out room keys and directing people to the hotel's clubhouse. In between answering questions and speaking with rescue workers, she tried calling her mother. The lack of answer ratcheted up her mounting anxiety. Was her mother safe?

"Julia, dear." Richard's words pulled her back to into the moment. "Mr. Sutton is pretty badly injured," he said of Wolfe Winery's owner. "The paramedics are ready to transport him to the hospital now."

"I need to see him." She followed him out to the waiting ambulance.

So far, he was the only person injured badly enough to require hospitalization—a damned lucky thing considering there were over two hundred souls in the hotel at the time. She took the man's hand. "Has someone contacted Cristobel?"

"I called her," Richard answered. "She's flying up on the next flight," he said of the man's wife and member of her mother's bridge club.

"I'm so sorry, Topher," she said to the middle-aged man she'd known most of her life. "I'll check up on you as soon as I can."

The man nodded before the paramedics slid the stretcher inside and closed the doors. Though he'd been a guest of the bride's family, she couldn't help feeling responsible for his presence at the wedding. Having learned the Alexanders had invited her neighbor, she'd arranged to have a meeting with him following the reception.

As she turned to head back inside, Richard stilled her with a hand to her arm. "Don't apologize to people." His lips thinned.

The criticism heated her cheeks. "Don't be ridiculous. I'm expressing sympathy not accepting responsibility. I may be a control freak, but even I know there's no controlling the weather."

"All the same. You shouldn't open yourself up to liability." He took her hand. "I know these people are your friends, but you should still be careful."

"They would never…"

"I'm only looking after your best interest."

"I understand." She tugged free from his grasp then headed back inside. Was Richard interested in more than an investment? Or was his hands-on approach part of his personality?

Before she could return inside, Libby met her under the *porte-cochére*. "The bride and groom want access to their suite to collect their luggage."

"Absolutely not until the fire department tells me the upper floors are safe."

"They're insisting." Libby bit her lip. "They want to leave for their honeymoon."

They'd also insisted they wanted the wedding in the field outside—and we see how well that worked out for them.

She couldn't fault them for wanting to escape the nightmare. "Let me get the all-clear first."

As Julia scanned the rescue vehicle-strewn parking lot for the fire chief, her gazed landed on the stable's roof just barely visible on the far side of a small knoll. Her barn manager, Joe-Lee, sent word the structure was fine, but she ached to check on D'Artagnan and the mares. Her horses were more than parts of her business or even pets. They were members of her family.

"Ms. Wilkes," Libby prompted. "What shall I tell the bride and groom?"

"Tell them I'll see them as soon as I can." Responsibility pulled her in a million directions. After tending to dozens of requests, both reasonable and downright dangerous, she slipped away to her first-floor suite to change into clothes more suitable for a disaster than the dress she been wearing. Just as she tugged on a pair of boots, her phone rang. Her pulse soared seeing Paul's number on the screen. "How's Aiden?"

"Not a scratch on him, but it took me a while to calm him down after the stormed passed. He's been asking for you."

"Put him on." Tears choked her voice. Ordinarily they used Facetime, but the last thing she wanted was for Aiden to see her cry.

"In just a moment," Paul said. "I need to tell you something first."

Her heart seized. "Is it my mother?"

"She's going to be okay—"

"Just tell me what's wrong."

"From what I can gather, she was trying to save a couple paintings and fell getting down to the wine cellar and broke her leg. She's at the hospital. My mom is with her and said the doctors want to keep her."

Julia let out a breath. Leave it to the historical society's president to value the family's heirlooms over her own safety. "I'll get down there as soon as I can, but it might be tomorrow. I still have people here I need to look after."

"I'll pass that along, but Mom said she'll stay as

long as necessary."

"Tell Teresa 'thank you' for me," she said, feeling if she was pulled in any more directions, she'd splinter apart. The urge to check out of this nightmare nearly overwhelmed her. That wasn't the type of person she wanted to be anymore. It might be a relief to take a break from responsibility occasionally, but a lifetime of escape led to an empty one. Not so long ago, a day like this one would have slayed her. Heck, even a small mishap was enough to send Old Julia to bed with a cold compress and a Xanax.

"Let me talk to Aiden now." She needed to connect with the center of her world.

"He's here."

Julia tamped down on her emotions. "Hi, sweetheart. Mommy misses you."

"I relayed the message and he's signing home."

She brushed away tears from her cheeks. "Tell him that I want to come get him, but I can't right now. Explain that the storm you had down in Atlanta was up here, too. It broke a lot of things, so I have to stay here to fix them."

"Sent and received. He's signing Pumpkin," Paul said, talking about the pony he'd purchased for their son's fourth birthday.

"I haven't been able to check on Pumpkin yet, but I bet he and the other horses are doing just fine."

"He's signing Pumpkin and food."

Julia chuckled, a touch of joy punctuating a truly unhappy day. "I gave him his oats and a carrot this morning."

There was a pause before Paul came back on the line. "I guess that's all he wanted to know. He just tore off for the playroom."

"Okay, I'll talk to you later." She mentally added items to her mile-long to-do list.

"Hold up," Paul said before she could end the call. "Have you been in touch with your insurance agent?"

She rolled her eyes. "I put a call into him an hour ago." Not even divorce could keep Paul Wilkes from trying to fix things for her. "I know you're dying to ask, so I'll go ahead and tell you. I'm fully insured, and I don't need your help."

"I didn't mean to imply you weren't competent to run your own business." He took the same placating tone one might use with a toddler. "I'm speaking one entrepreneur to another."

Paul had been her biggest supporter when she announced her intention to purchase the resort, but she'd been far too reliant on him emotionally and financially during their marriage. She wouldn't revert to old habits even if it meant the difference between her business' success and failure. "Thank you for your concern. So, from one business owner to another, how'd your business make out in the storm?"

"Jeez, you don't even want to know. I'll be digging out of that mess for months."

"I'm sorry to hear that." Someone rapped on her door. "Listen, I've got to go, but I'll check back later tonight." Julia ended the call and returned to the battle scene that had once been her beautiful resort.

Chapter Three

Julia let out a breath as the last rescue vehicle zigzagged its way down the drive. All the wedding guests who chose to stay were bedded down in the undamaged rooms and the more daring had ventured onto the tree-strewn roads, including Richard.

Thank God.

Now, she could finally head down to the barn to check on her horses.

She picked her way through rubble-strewn lawn, stepping over a heap of lumber that had once been the fence separating the hotel from the pasture.

"Where are you going?"

Luke's baritone voice resonated deep inside her and stopped her breath, stopped her next step, stopped her heart. "To the barn. To check on my horses." She turned to face him, working hard not to let his harsh appearance affect her. He'd been a handsome man in his twenties, but it appeared time had chiseled his features to angled perfection, even the skull trim and piercings couldn't detract from his god-like face. The day's events, however, had taken their toll. Veins threaded the whites of his eyes like a road map.

She clenched her hand to rein in the urge to smooth the creases of fatigue around his generous mouth. "You look done in. See Rachel at the front desk, and she'll get you set up with a room."

"No need, ma'am. I'm headed out soon."

Ma'am?

She refused to play along with his game of denial. "Thank you for taking care of my guests. Who knew a veterinary education would come so in handy?"

His expression darkened.

Exhausted, she didn't have the energy to press him to acknowledge her. She turned her back on him and headed toward the barn. He fell in alongside her. "You don't have to follow me. I know to be careful."

"Do you?" He continued with her down the slope that blocked the view of the barn from the hotel.

Her first unimpeded view of the barn nearly brought her to her knees. "Dear God."

Clearly, her definition of fine and Joe-Lee's differed. The tin roof was pealed back, exposing everything inside to the elements. Bales of hay blew across the demolished training ring where Aiden rode Pumpkin. Worst of all, the corner where the pony's stall had collapsed. The place wasn't even in the same zip code as fine. Panic added speed to her steps. "No!"

As she rushed headlong toward the barn, Luke easily matched her pace. "Watch out." Luke lifted her off her feet so that she missed stepping on a nail jutting from an upturned board. He held her for a moment longer before setting her back on her feet. Now her heart raced for a completely different reason. "Thank you. Maybe I do need someone down here with me."

His brow furrowed as if he was fighting a battle with himself. "Right." He pointed to the near side of the barn. "Let's start on this end and work our way around. I want to check out the structure before we go inside."

Side-by-side, they walked the perimeter coming to

the most damaged part of the barn last. “Pumpkin.” Fear of what she’d find inside tangled her insides.

“Let me look for you.”

Julia held her breath, praying the animal hadn’t suffered.

“It’s empty.”

A laugh escaped her throat as relief spread through her. “For once I’m glad our little guy is a Houdini. Can’t keep him in his stall when he wants the pasture. I’ve tried everything I know to do short of nailing him in, and he always manages to break free.”

“It looks safe when you’re ready to check on the rest.”

Entering through the gaping hole where the barn door once had been, she made her way down the center, looking at each animal. She cooed and petted her rescues, offering them each a sugar cube from the stash in her pocket.

Luke hung back, but she was aware of him watching her every move as if he expected some danger to leap out at her. As they neared the last stall he finally spoke. “They’re a motley looking crew.”

She jerked around, planting her fists on her hips. “I’ll have you know, they’re a good herd. I trained them myself. Not a biter, bucker, or runner in the bunch. I’d let my son ride any one of them.”

He held up his hands in surrender. “Take it easy, princess. I take it back.”

Before she could say any more, D’Artagnan called for her—in his usual way, by kicking the side of his stall. “I’m coming, boy.”

She stalked off, still offended by Luke’s comment. She couldn’t afford the pedigreed horses like his family owned. "Take it easy. I'm here." She reached through the bars and was rewarded with a love nip. Her boy was the exception in her well-mannered group, both in appearance and temperament. The handsome Selle Français had been a challenge to gentle, and he begrudgingly accepted her on his back.

After offering him a sweet from her pocket, she flipped the latch on his stall. She'd put a foot across the threshold when Luke grabbed her by the waist.

"You're not going in there. That animal looks like he'd just as soon stomp you as to look at you."

She rounded on him. "What's up with you telling me what to do? It's been like that since you ran down my hallway this morning." She kicked up her chin to meet his gaze. "At one time, I might have appreciated someone protecting me, but I've grown up a lot since we last saw each other. I know how to take care of myself." She also knew to protect her heart.

He pushed the stall door closed before setting her on her feet again. "I'm not so sure about that. Remember the four-inch nail you nearly stepped on? And I believe you were headed out into the tornado when we met in your hotel."

Ignoring him, she yanked open D'Artagnan's door and stepped inside. "Easy, boy," she murmured when he backed his ears. "You've had a rough couple hours, haven't you?" She ran her hands over his flanks and down his legs, checking for injury.

Seeing that he was fine, she crossed to the other side of the barn to the tack room. Luke's gaze followed her, though he stayed out of her way. She gave the door a hard pull, but it wouldn't budge. She tried several more times with no success.

"Will you let me help with that?"

"Actually, that would be great." She stepped out of the way. "I may be stubborn, but I'm not stupid."

He jerked it opened to reveal thousands of dollars' worth of tack broken beneath the collapsed roof. "What a wreck." She shook her head. "Looks to be a total loss."

"I'm sorry for your troubles."

She swallowed passed the lump in her throat. "Thank you." Then she dug around in the mess for a feed bucket. Once she finally pried one loose, she wiped the inside with her hand and began searching for a lead line.

"I never expected to see you willing to get your hands dirty. No offense, but the Julia I knew was a vastly different girl."

She chuckled. "None taken. I know what I used to be like. The only thing I ever wielded was a credit card. I'm full of surprises. My life has changed a great deal in the past decade, most of it in just the last couple years.

Julia glanced out the window to the west. "Now that I've got everyone in here secured, I need to look for Pumpkin." She grabbed the length of rope then filled a bucket with sweet feed. "Lord, I hope he didn't get tangled up in the blackberry bushes again like he did during a thunderstorm last summer." Then she looked around, trying to predict what else she might need. She grabbed a folding knife and flashlight and set out in search of the pony.

"It's too dangerous out there. The pasture's got to be covered with debris. Why don't you wait to see if he shows up on his own?"

Julia shook her head. "I can't. He could be hurt."

She nodded toward the hotel. "I told my assistant, Rachel, to save you a room. We don't have hot water, but you can clean up a little and get some sleep."

Luke stared at his feet. "I thought I'd head out."

"Now who's being stubborn? You're going to get on roads that are impassable at worst and a minefield of junk at best."

"You make a good point." He continued following her into the pasture.

She turned to look over her shoulder. "I know my land better than I know my way around Nordstrom's. You don't have to come with me."

"Just keeping you company."

Julia trekked to the obvious place first, a small grove of trees that would offer the pony some protection. "Pumpkin." She banged the plastic bucket against her thigh. "Come here, buddy. Mama's got your favorite."

After she checked several other places the pony could have found shelter, she finally caught sight of a familiar shade of brown. Heart racing faster than her feet carried her, she sprinted toward the pony, which lay on his side.

Luke caught her arm as she tugged at a large branch pinning the animal to the ground. "There's nothing you can do for him. He's gone."

"I see his sides moving." She wrenched away. Her gut clenched. "Oh, my sweet, boy." Julia cradled his head in her lap. "What happened to you?" She couldn't, couldn't, couldn't lose her son's pony. He'd been a wonderful addition to their family, bringing so much joy to Aiden's life. "My son adores his pony. Please, please do something for him."

She'd seen Luke nurse a horse back from colic when others thought it should be put down. "I have supplies and medicine back in the tack room that my vet left for one of the horses. Go get that."

"It's too late. He's dying."

Her failures overwhelmed her. Why hadn't she seen to the animals herself? "He can't." She choked back a sob. "I won't let that happen."

After removing the branch, Luke ran a hand along the animal's flank. "His breathing is labored, and his pulse is rapid."

"Is he in pain?"

"Probably."

She swallowed hard. "Do you have a revolver? I don't keep a gun around because of my son, but if you have one, I'll do it. I don't want him suffering."

"No, I don't, but it's not necessary anyway. He's leaving us, now."

Julia petted Pumpkin's head and neck. "You go to that wide-open pasture you see. No more fences and stalls for you. Nothing but sweet grass, oats, and sugar cubes." Finally, the animal closed his eyes and let out a final breath.

Luke wrapped his arms around her, rocking her slowly. "I'm so sorry, Julia."

She buried her face in his chest. "It's my fault. I should have done more to keep him safe."

"That's not true." He turned her face to his. "We can't always keep what we love safe, no matter how much we try."

"But he was my responsibility." The failure lanced through her.

"You can't control everything." He tugged her to

her feet. "There's nothing more we can do here. Let's go back to the hotel. We can take care of the pony in the morning."

Julia dug in her heels as he tried to lead her away. "I can't leave him like this."

Luke let out a breath. "Okay then. I'll see what I can find back at the barn to bury him."

The need for independence warred with her desire not to abandon the animal who'd meant so much to Aiden. "There's a backhoe in the shed beside the clubhouse. The keys are on the pegboard."

His jaw ticked. "I'll be back as soon as I can." Then he was off at a trot, leaving her alone with her thoughts.

As she awaited Luke's return, her thoughts rolled back a dozen years. They'd been each other's first, and she'd been utterly in love, despite their differences. It had taken years of furtive glances and awkward conversations for their crush to blossom. When it did, in the summer before her senior year of college, Julia had thought it would last forever.

The rumbling sound of the backhoe pulled her back to the here and now. Luke came alongside her, not quite touching. "I brought back help, so you don't have to stay. Why don't you go back to the hotel?"

When her father died, Paul had been the one to make the arrangements. She'd relied completely on him for every decision. While the death of a pet wasn't on par with losing her father, she wouldn't foist this responsibility on to another. "I need to stay. They can spare me back at the hotel a little while longer."

As the groundskeeper began working, Luke reached for her hand. A surge of electricity shot up her arm. She longed to bury herself in his embrace but taking comfort in his strong arms would only lead to heartache. If his past was any indication, he'd disappear without notice again.

Rain began falling. "Here, take my coat." He wrapped it around her shoulders. The leather mixed with clean sweat and overwhelmed her senses. She brought her nose to the collar and breathed in the scent. For a moment, she was no longer standing graveside amid a disaster. She was the Julia of old, the girl who dreamed of happily-ever-after and saw no reason why her wishes wouldn't come true.

Julia stood silently inches from him until the backhoe did its job and trundled into the darkness.

"We should get inside." Luke pointed to the hotel.

"You go ahead. I'll be up in a moment."

He shot her a look, patient yet unyielding. "I'll check on the horses then come back to get you."

She trusted few with her four-legged babies, same as with her son. Her heart twinge, remembering the all-too-soon conversation she needed to have. Was six years of age old enough to understand death? "Thank you. Would you please check that Misty hasn't overturned her water?"

He nodded before leaving her side.

Julia keenly felt the loss of him. She couldn't do this on her own, couldn't face the destruction. The familiar urge to run overwhelmed her. She ripped self-doubt from her thoughts as ruthlessly as she did weeds from her roses. She'd failed the little pony, but she wouldn't fail the others who relied on her, animal and human alike.

With a quick prayer of thanks for the animal who'd

brought such joy to her son's life, Julia prodded herself into action. "Hold up. I'll come with you."

He shortened his stride, so she was able to catch up. "I might not be a vet anymore, but I think I'm capable of running a garden hose," he said without censure.

"I'm sure you are, but D'Artagnan won't let anyone but me near him."

Luke muttered something that sounded an awful lot like, "smart boy." With the wind whipping around them, she couldn't be certain.

In between calls from the hotel staff needing her to smooth out issues, they bedded the horses down for the night. After midnight, Luke dusted the last of the hay from his hands. "I think we've both earned a little rest."

"You'll stay?" She was unable to keep the surprise from her voice. Even as he'd helped her feed the horses, he seemed to have one foot out the door.

"Probably for the best. As you said before, the roads are bad. I can sleep on the floor somewhere. From the looks of things, there might not be any rooms left undamaged. I know you need to take care of your guests first."

Julia intended to offer her suite, but the moment she stepped inside the lobby, she was bombarded by people. As employees and guests peppered her with questions, she searched the space for him. Nothing. How could a man, so large and imposing, disappear that quickly?

****

The next morning, Luke traced a finger along the deep scratch running the length of his bike's fuel tank. That was it—the extent of the damaged it suffered.

He'd caught a break on that one, needing to get far away from Julia and the memories she stirred up. He adjusted the strap on one of the saddlebags then cast an eye across her property. It would be months before she had Highlands up and running again, but as she'd said at least half a dozen times yesterday, she could handle her own problems. Yet, he couldn't make himself leave. She'd changed over the years, and he longed to know the woman she'd become.

He'd stalled as much as he could, waking before dawn to repair the corral so her horses would have a safe place until she found somewhere to board them.

He rubbed his chest trying to massage the ache inside. For the sake of his sanity, he needed to get far away from the town, away from the memories, away from Julia. Memories he'd kept locked away broke open as he'd held her in his arms. Once free, they rushed back with painful clarity.

Instead of swinging a leg over his bike, he took the few steps into the lobby. No harm in a quick goodbye. His thoughts rewound to their last parting. It had been at the beginning of his final year in vet school. She was returning to Sweet Briar College. He'd promised to call the next day. A phone call from his sister changed all that and rendered his promise impossible to keep.

He looked around the lobby for Julia, without success. Finally, he found her second-in-command. "Excuse me." The brunette looked dead on her feet. "Can you tell me where Julia is?"

She narrowed her green eyes, scanning him from head to toe. "If you're a guest, sir, I can help you."

"I'm not. I took shelter during the storm yesterday. I wanted to tell Julia goodbye."

The woman folded her arms across her chest. "She's busy, as you can imagine. I'll be glad to pass on your message."

"No thanks." It was just as well considering he wasn't sure he had the strength to resist if she asked him to stay.

"Drive safely."

"One thing," he called out to her as several people approached.

She arched an eyebrow.

"Look after Julia, will you? Be sure she eats. She tends to forget when she gets busy."

Her lips compressed. "I'll do that." She then turned to address a woman still dressed for yesterday's wedding.

Back outside, Luke threw his leg over the bike then kicked the engine to life. Rescue crews had cleared the road, allowing him to open the throttle on his way out. One quick stop to check on his new property and he'd be back in Ohio by nightfall.

Luke slowed as he passed the barn. Still regretting the way he'd shut down her questions, he wanted to offer a token apology. He owed her much more. But that would never happen. He couldn't risk her knowing the truth.

He edged his bike to the side of the road. After leaping over the top of the fence, he picked his way to the barn. "Julia." When she didn't answer his calls, he suspected where he'd find her. As he crossed the corral, one of the horses approached.

"Hey there, girl." He gave the horse's pall a good scratch. The animal leaned into his hand. "Been a rough night, huh." He loved all animals, but horses had an especially soft place in his heart. At one time, when he'd had his life mapped out, he'd seen Julia and him owning a large ranch. They'd talked about moving out west. He'd open a practice while she'd run a riding school.

Clearly, her plans had altered along the way. Did she ever think about what might have been?

He shook himself out of the doldrums. Though construction didn't bring the happiness veterinary medicine would, it allowed him to accomplish the goal he'd set for himself.

His builder's eye studied the metal structure. She'd probably be better off razing the barn than trying to repair the damage. He stopped calculating the cost in his head. It was none of his business what she did. And he couldn't stay. Surely there were others who could help her shoulder the burden, like that fancy guy who'd been with her yesterday.

Richie Rich was in a much better position to help. All Luke could do was bring her down, especially if anyone investigated his past. Court documents were open record, and Alabama wasn't that far away.

With a final pat on the horse's flank, he walked over the low hill to where he'd find Julia. Her light-blonde hair stood out amongst the bright green of the bushes surrounding her as she knelt over the fresh grave.

She brushed away tears as he hunkered down beside her. "You heading out?"

"Yeah." He'd seen her dressed in designer gowns and riding habits, but she blew him away dressed in worn jeans and a sweatshirt with her hair blowing freely and the wind pinking her cheeks.

"Any chance I can convince you to stay a day or two?" She looked up at him with pleading eyes. "I'd love to find out what you've been doing with yourself all these years."

Which was exactly why he couldn't remain.

His past needed to stay where it was, and his present wasn't anything to talk about—work, sleep, repeat. Been that way since he left Alabama. Couple times a year, he got together with his sister, but that was the extent of his social life. He'd been okay with that until now. Julia stirred something inside him. "Sorry, no. I have work tomorrow."

She stood, dusting her hands against her jeans. "Thanks for lending your skills yesterday."

"It wasn't much."

She drew closer, sending his pulse racing as he caught her delicate scent. "Don't say that. I don't know how I would have gotten through last night if it weren't for you."

"Rescuers would have gotten to your guests before too long."

She glanced over her shoulder to the mound of red Georgia earth. "I'm not talking about the hotel. I needed to be with someone who understands how important these animals are to me."

"Again, it was nothing. I'm sure your boyfriend would have done the same."

"Boyfriend?" Her brows arched.

"That guy you were went in the ballroom."

"Oh, you mean Richard Pierce. Definitely not my boyfriend. He's a capital investor who was going to help me expand my resort. He wouldn't be caught dead in a barn. In fact, he advised me to do away with the stables." She took his hand, lacing her fingers with his. "You showing up here after all these years feels like a dream. You never did say why you came back."

Her touch licked up his arm, making it difficult to string together his words. "Had some…unfinished business…to handle." He wished he'd been able to present his mother with the deed to the farm before she died last year.

"Will you be coming back to Magnolia Valley anytime soon?"

"Don't think so." All the particulars of closing on the property could be handled over email.

Julia stepped up to his body, her slender arms going around him. "I guess this is it."

He couldn't stay and keep his sanity. Couldn't watch her and not want to take her or explain what happened. If he were the gentleman she deserved, he'd push her away. At best, he'd been a country vet with dirt under his nails and shit on his boots. He wasn't even that much now; just an ex-con trying to eke out a living.

He could allow this one indulgence. "This is how it has to be." Then he kissed her. Tender at first but growing more intense as she responded. When they finally broke the kiss, both were breathless.

"Take care of yourself, princess." He turned away from her, striding across the open field as fast as his legs could take him. Not since the early days after the Unfortunate Event, as his mother called it, had he grieved so hard for what he'd lost.

Chapter Four

Julia pressed her fingers to her lips. He'd kissed her senseless then walked away as if nothing happened. She willed him to look back, wanting one more glance at his brutally handsome face. But why? Luke Chevalier had the potential to do as much damage to her heart as the tornado had done to her business. Instead of obeying her silent plea, he strode across the pasture until he crested the hill and disappeared out of sight.

"Stop. Being. Stupid." The late-March wind whisked her angry words away. She tugged her jacket closely around her and headed back to the hotel. "You've got enough to think about without digging up the past."

Reaching her office, she found Rachel loading documents from the filing cabinet into plastic bins. The fire chief declared the building safe enough for them to clear out her office, and the remaining guests were leaving that morning.

Rachel glanced up from her work, looking as tired as Julia felt. "Some guy was looking for you earlier."

"He found me." She kept her voice even in hopes of preventing her friend from sensing the tumult of emotions churning inside her.

"Just who is he anyway?"

Julia should have known better than try to fool the

woman who could spot a diversion tactic at a thousand paces. "Just someone I used to know. Someone who happened to be passing through when the storm struck."

Someone who was the heartbreak of my past.

Rachel cocked her head. "Didn't know you hung out with people like that. He looks dangerous."

"He didn't look like that when I knew him." She opened a desk drawer and began unloading office supplies into another of the bins.

"I sense a love story there."

Julia gave up trying to downplay the impact Luke had on her life. "At one point I thought so." She shrugged. "I was wrong. Ours was more like a tragedy."

"Speaking of that, I'm sorry about the pony." Her friend placed a hand on Julia's shoulder. "You have to know it wasn't your fault."

She widened her eyes to keep the tears from falling. "Doesn't feel that way." Swallowing past the lump in her throat, she changed the subject. "Did you get some rest?"

Rachel waved away her concern. "You know I don't need much sleep. I took a catnap earlier." She pointed to the dark circles beneath Julia's eyes. "I don't need to ask if your head ever touched a pillow."

"I guess having chronic insomnia has its perks." She chuckled. Their paths often crossed in the wee hours of the night. "Where do we stand on supplies this morning?"

"You want the good news first or the bad?"

"Good news. I already know the bad." Or at least she had a fairly good idea of the extent of damage. She'd have a better sense once she finally got a contractor to look at the place.

"Chef says the clubhouse kitchen is operational. He's got enough provisions to give the guests breakfast."

"Excellent." Her phone rang, and seeing the caller was one of the eight contractors she'd contacted, she quickly swiped to accept the call. "Mr. Patrick, please tell me you can give me an estimate."

"I can get up to your place in an hour."

Her gaze shot skyward. "You're a Godsend." Had her run of misfortune reached an end?

****

Luke turned right at the end of Highlands's drive. Before hitting the highway, he needed to check on Rockaway Farm, the name that would once again grace the fifty acres of rolling pastureland. As he traveled the distance separating the two tracts of land, tension coiled inside him. Twisted metal and pink insolation hung from the bare oak limbs like a sick version of Christmas trees.

He topped the hill and let out a breath. Tree limbs littered the front yard and a few dark-green roof shingles had blown loose. That was the extent of the damage. The contrast to Julia's place sent a twinge of guilt running through him.

After making a quick call to the realtor explaining what he planned to do and assuring her he meant to go through with the sale, he got to work. Thanks to the saw and hammer he found in the old tool shed.

With the minor repairs made, he wandered down to the stable. Wind whistled through the empty space, stirring up the wood shavings that covered the floor. A hundred memories flooded back as he walked the length of the central hallway. All the milestones of his young life happened within those walls or were influenced by the goings on within the wood and stone structure.

His parents had emigrated from France in the 1970s, bringing with them Selle Français breeding stock. Then they'd gone about establishing a national reputation as expert breeders and trainers of the majestic saddle horse. His upbringing had been a blend of influences from his parents' homeland and their love of all things American.

Julia Chandler came into their lives when her father purchased one of Rockaway's three-year-olds and hired the Chevaliers to train him. He could still see a teenaged Julia astride the spirited animal. Her quiet confidence attracted him as much as her beauty had. Over the course of his visits home from college and his acceptance to veterinary school, he'd fallen in love with her without them sharing more than a handful of conversations.

Finally, when he mustered the courage to act on his feelings, they'd had only a few months to explore their love before that fateful phone call from his sister.

He moved from stall to empty stall, envisioning it once again filled with sights, sounds, and scents of animals. "Ah jeez."

He scrubbed his palm over his skull trim. It made no sense for Julia's horses to stay in a damaged barn while his stood empty. Putting things right would be the work of a moment.

His hand went to his hip pocket, but he didn't have her contact information. Hell, who was he kidding? Even if he had her number, he'd want to see her expression when he made the offer. He so rarely got to do something good; he couldn't resist getting the reward of making her happy. It would delay him reaching Ohio but only by a few hours. He still had time to bid on the project outside Cincinnati by late afternoon Monday.

Back at Highlands, he spotted Julia next to a truck with *Paddy and Sons Contracting* painted on the side. Next to her, dressed in overalls and holding a clipboard had, to be the proprietor. As he approached, her eyes widened momentarily before she turned her attention back to the man who was pointing to various areas of damage to her hotel. Luke hung back to eavesdrop. He'd seen unscrupulous contractors descend after a disaster like turkey buzzards on a fresh carcass.

"You'll be using top grade materials, right? None of that junk from China I've heard about?"

Luke wanted to cheer. She was doing her homework. He wasn't surprised, though. Of all the things one could call this beautiful woman, pushover wasn't one of them.

"Don't you worry about a thing, missy. I'll use nothing but the best on your place."

She pressed her lips together, making him wonder if the contractor realized how close he was to catching hell for his condescension.

"And you can meet my timeline as well? Wedding season is coming up, and I need to be operational by the first week in June."

The balding man in his late fifties waved away her concern. "Not a problem. Don't you worry your pretty little head about a thing. I'll have your place done in no time."

Her jaw ticked. "When can you give me an

estimate?"

The man scribbled something on a piece of paper, tore it off the pad and passed it to her. "I'll write up a formal estimate, but here's a rough number."

Her eyes widened. "That much, Paddy?"

"That's what it's going to take. These kinds of repairs don't come cheap."

Her shoulders slumped. "How soon can you begin?"

"I can have a crew on site this afternoon. All I need is a check for twenty thousand up front."

Luke had heard enough. Julia had asked all the right questions, but this guy was a rip-off pro. He stormed over to her, took the paper out of her hands, and thrust it back at the contractor. "Get out of here."

"What are you doing, Luke?" She reached around him for the estimate. "I need this guy."

"He's overcharging you."

She shot Paddy a look. "I know exactly what he was doing, but he's the only one who'd come out." She pointed to the gaping hole where the hotel's front doors had once been. "It's supposed to rain later today, and the damage will only get worse."

"Listen, lady, I got five calls this morning for my services. If you don't think you're getting a good deal, I've got places to be."

Julia held up a finger. "Just give me a moment, please." She took Luke by the sleeve and yanked him out of the contractor's earshot. "I know this guy is overcharging me." She lowered her voice. "But he's also got me backed into a corner. I've got weddings booked every weekend through the rest of the year. As it is, I'll have to cancel at least ten of them. With the summer vacation season coming, I can't afford to lose that business."

His hand ached to sooth the tension from her face. "Take a moment to get some other bids," he urged, instead of acting on his body's demands and taking her into his arms.

She planted her fists on her hips. "What do you want me to do, let the rain do more damage? I don't have much choice short of grabbing a hammer myself."

"I'll do it." The words were out before he could talk himself out of making the offer. "I can get my crew down here by late-Tuesday. In the meantime, I'll go into town for some tarps." The job he'd planned to bid on tomorrow was nothing spectacular and the crew he employed was rootless like him.

Her hand flew to her mouth. "You'd do that for me?"

"For you, princess, I'd do anything." His gut tightened as self-preservation played catchup to his mouth.

How in the hell had he arrived planning to offer her a place to board her horses, and in the span of a few impulsive minutes, managed to ensnare himself in her world? He scrubbed his head. Staying ahead of the questions that would surely come would be a feat on par with keeping his bike upright in that tornado. He gazed into her lovely face, and the relief he saw made his chest swell. Fuck the questions. He had bigger issues, like seeing her every day and not acting on the lust coursing through his veins.

Julia held up a finger. "Stay right there."

Her smile lit up his insides.

"I'll send dirt bag on his way."

"Not going anywhere." Especially if he got to be the one to keep that expression on her face.

****

A few days after the tornado, Julia returned to her mother's hospital room. Teresa Wilkes, her mother's best friend and Julia's former mother-in-law, sat next to the bed. The two spoke in hushed tones, so engrossed in conversation they didn't notice she'd entered. Perhaps, if these were any other late-middle-aged women, a person might suppose they were planning a vacation, shopping trip, or even gossiping about the other well-to-do families in Atlanta. But, no, these two were plotting.

Her sympathies lay with the subject of their scheme. "Good morning." She smoothed her hand over the pale pink button-down shirt she'd paired with jeans.

They jolted at her greeting.

"Good morning, yourself," Teresa said at the same time her mother said, "Hello, my darling." The friends trained their butter-wouldn't-melt-in-my-mouth smiles on her.

Ah, so I'm the one in their crosshairs.

"How are you feeling today, Mother?" Julia walked over to give her a gentle hug before pressing a kiss to Mrs. Wilkes' cheek. "Teresa, you're looking well. Has the doctor been in yet? I was hoping to catch him today."

In addition to visiting her mother in the Atlanta hospital each day, she'd also been dealing with an insurance company dragging its feet, saying goodbye to faithful employees, and finding a place to live.

"No, he hasn't." Teresa cast her gaze the length of Julia. "Although I'm surprised if you were planning to catch him, you didn't dress up a bit more. Men are visual creatures, my dear. He needs to see you at your best, not looking like you've come from the barn."

Lovely smile, gentle voice, spine of steel.

After the divorce and Paul's marriage to Michelle almost two years ago, she hoped Teresa would have finally given up her meddling. "That's not why I want to see him." Julia picked at her short, bare nails. She hardly had time for a shower much less time to change into a dress before visiting. Even before the tornado, dating hadn't been a priority.

"I need to discuss our options regarding Mother's release from the hospital."

"Paul said you should send me to St. Anne's Terrace. It has a luxury rehabilitation wing for seniors."

Her ex-husband sure liked to offer a good deal of advice. When it came to business, she was open to suggestions. This, however, crossed a line. "Why have you been consulting him?"

She took a deep breath and reminded herself Paul didn't know how little money she had on hand, and she planned to keep it that way. If he learned about her financial situation, he'd insist on paying for everything.

No one else knew what Julia discovered after her father's death. In the span of a generation, thanks to her father's poor investment choices and her mother's outrageous shopping habit, they'd burned through two family fortunes.

Helene raised her chin. "It came up during his daily visit. He's only looking after me."

"This is none of his business." Julia wished she could make her mother grasp their situation. Make her consider downsizing. Make her stick to a budget. No one *made* Helene do anything. Julia had tried, though. Not long after her father's death, she brought up the family's dwindling fortunes. Her mother flatly refused to even discuss money, calling it a vulgar, middle-class topic. More likely, having come from one of Atlanta's richest families, the concept of frugality was beyond her comprehension.

"You're my responsibility, not his. I've got the divorce decree to prove it."

Her mother stiffened. "I'm sorry I'm such a burden. I suppose you might as well put me in a nursing home."

Manipulating much, Mother?

Not only was Helene Ansley Chandler queen of denial, but she'd also achieved a master's rank in the art of guilt. If anyone else tried to pull something like this, Julia would have called them out. Things were different with her mother.

She sunk to the bed and took her hand. "No one said anything about a nursing home. Worse case, you'll go to the hospital's rehabilitation center until I can rent a suitable house for us."

"I still don't understand why I can't go back to Oakton." Her whining better fit that of a petulant child than a mature woman. "Just have someone install a hospital bed in your father's study."

Yet another responsibility landed on her shoulders. The Ansley ancestral home had needed extensive repairs before the tornado. She'd hoped the expansion of Highlands would generate enough profits to pay for the renovation. With the added damage from the tornado, it might never be financially feasible to restore one of Atlanta's oldest private homes to its former glory. As it was now, the mansion built in 1893 by Frederick Law Olmsted wasn't inhabitable.

"Going back to Oakton isn't a possibility for the same reason having you up to the resort won't work. It's simply not safe."

"Why can't I stay with you?"

A laugh escaped Julia's lips before she could catch it. "You'd stay with me at the Magnolia Inn?" The motel where she was staying until she could find a place to rent had two important attributes; it was clean and cheap. "There's no room service, and you can hear trucks going down the highway all night."

Her mother's eyes widened. "Certainly not."

"Where I'm staying isn't an option, either," Teresa chimed in. "I'm staying with Paul and Michelle in Decatur." The woman made the bungalow in the historic neighborhood sound like a double-wide, something she would be familiar with if she cared to remember. By the time Julia and Paul married, he was well on his way to making his company a success, and Teresa had already shed her working-class mantle.

"That place is simply impossible. We're in there cheek by jowl."

"It's all temporary. Millions of people live under worse conditions. I'm looking at a place today that has three bedrooms, one of them downstairs." She turned to her former mother-in-law. "If Mother and I share, there'll be enough room for you to join us."

Teresa's face lit up. "What a wonderful idea. This will be such great fun." The septuagenarian clapped her hands like a child at a birthday party. "I'll tell Paul when I see him tonight."

A smile tugged at the corner of Julia's lip as she

made a mental note to remind Paul he owed her a favor for taking Teresa off his hands. Before they could discuss any of the plans, a rap came on the door and the doctor entered.

Helene sat up, adjusting her bed jacket. "Hello, Dr. Melton. You remember my daughter, Julia."

The man in his early forties with refined features and nary a sign of grey hair extended his hand to her. "Of course, what a pleasure to see you again. Your mother tells me you're busy rebuilding your business." He pushed his wire-rimmed glasses higher on his nose. "I do hope you're being cautious. I've seen a lot of injuries related to the storm." He was handsome in an academic sort of way, the type of well-to-do professional her mother would choose for her. He looked a lot like Richard, with his expensive clothes and polished manners. She tried to find the type attractive, but nothing about their smooth ways stirred her.

Still, she fidgeted under the doctor's assessing gaze, smoothing a hand over her shirt, a nervous habit from when she'd endured uniform inspections at school. "I am quite careful, thank you. I was hoping we could discuss my mother's discharge date."

Dr. Melton glanced at the chart. "I think she could be discharged tomorrow."

"That soon?" Panic set in. "I don't think I can find a house until the end of the week. We've all been displaced because of the tornado."

The doctor's gaze softened. "I think I can manage to keep her here until you find a place for her." He then turned his attention to her mother, discussing her recovery and patiently answering questions.

After he left, Julia leaned in to give her mother a hug. "I'll come back for a visit tomorrow, but I need to go if I'm going to see that place today. Teresa, I'll call Paul on my way. I'll let him know you're coming to stay with me. This will be fun. Just the four of us. It'll be like that vacation we took to the beach." Julia hoped she put a positive twist on what would no doubt be a challenging situation.

****

After closing on Rockaway Farm, Luke sat at a kitchen table left by the former owners. It hadn't taken more than half a morning to move his things in and unpack. "Hardly anything's changed," he said to his sister, Yvonne, over the phone. "The last owners painted downstairs, but that's about it. Even Mom's wallpaper with the roosters is still up in the kitchen."

His sister chuckled, something he rarely heard from her. "Do their eyes still follow you all over the room?"

He took a sip of coffee. "Pretty much." He studied the room with its heart of pine floors and aging appliances and didn't want to change a thing—except the Foghorn Leghorn wannabes, yeah; maybe it was time for them to come down.

"I'm so proud of you. When you told me a few years ago what you planned to do, I didn't believe it was possible. You did it though."

He cleared his throat. He hadn't survived Holman then worked eighteen-hour days the past five years for himself alone. "I want you and Jake to come live here. It's the perfect place to raise a kid."

She let out a breath. "Luke, no. I'm sorry. I can't. My life is here in Kansas now."

He tamped down on his disappointment. The last thing his sister needed was more guilt. Luke got up from his seat and placed the mug in the sink. The house beat the hell out of the trailer he'd been living in. However, it was a home meant for a family. "At lease come for a few days once Jake gets out of school."

Luke grabbed his keys, heading into the front yard. In the distance, the whine of an eighteen-wheeler disturbed the quiet. He'd found the silence a blessing the first few days back on the family farm. Now, it seemed to echo all that was lacking in his life.

It poised on his lips to tell his sister that all would be as it once had been. That was a delusion, even with the same chickens staring at him over his corn flakes or the stable filled with horses. Too much had happened. It could, however, be proof they could overcome that one horrific night.

"I'll bring him down for a visit."

"Good." The sun peeked over the mountain top, signaling it was time for him to wind his way over the six miles of twisted road to Highlands. "Listen, I've got to get to work."

"I can't believe you're working for Julia Chandler. Is she still the Ice Princess?"

He reined in the urge to come to Julia's defense. No sense in cueing his sister to how badly he still had it for her. Hell, he didn't want to admit to himself that he spent a good deal of his day thinking about the way her long hair brushed against the small of her back or the gentle blush that graced her cheeks.

He leaned against a fence post and stared at the empty pasture. It dawned on him he hadn't made the offer to board Julia's horses. He avoided her as much as possible, working when he knew she would be down in Atlanta visiting her mother, and setting his crew on their tasks then leaving on the days she worked at the resort. Maybe he could email her the offer.

"Tell me she's gotten fat and has crow's feet," Yvonne said, breaking into his thoughts.

"She's changed, just like all of us." For the better in his estimation. Actually, she was more beautiful than she'd been back in the day.

"Don't let her put you down and make sure she pays you up front. Her kind likes to think they don't have to play by the same rules as the rest of us, but she's wrong." Bitterness colored his sister's words. Yvonne had been jealous of Julia, longing for the expensive car and wardrobe the Chandler fortune could buy.

"Julia is a fair business owner. She cut me a check before I began work, and her stable of horses are all rescues."

"Don't you *dare* fall for her again."

Shock ran through him. He'd kept his love affair with Julia a secret. "How'd you know?"

"You two weren't as stealthy as you thought, brother mine." Her voice softened. "Promise me you'll watch yourself. I don't want you getting hurt."

He had no intention of acting on the renewed attraction. "Don't worry about me. If I can survive five years at Holman, I think I can handle being around Julia without getting scathed." He didn't worry she'd treat him unfairly. It was his growing desire for her he had to guard against. A good part of him wished he hadn't offered to rebuild her resort, but he'd never been one to walk away from someone in need.

"Listen, I really got to go. I'll talk to you again soon, Sis. Give Jake a hug and tell him Uncle Luke's going to get him the sweetest mare in the world for his city-boy-self to ride."

"I'll do that." Again, she chuckled, a veritable record for her. "Luke…" She paused. "Ah, about the farm, thanks. Even if I can't come live there, it means a lot knowing it's there for me. Mom and Dad would be proud of you."

A surge of triumph bubbled up. Too bad their parents hadn't lived long enough to see his accomplishment.

After he ended the call, Luke lingered in the paddock. He didn't share his sister's concerns about Julia's business dealings. The woman did have the potential to do damage to other areas. Without meaning to, she drew him in. Activated his need to protect, although she was perfectly capable of taking care of herself and everyone else in her life.

Maybe that was the draw, seeing her tend to everyone like a mother hen with her chicks. He needed to watch himself. The Ice Princess might have thawed, but it didn't change the fact he wasn't the same young man he'd once been.

So why was he working a plan that would draw her closer?

The wind caught the barn door, banging it shut. The presence of Julia's animals would ease the loneliness, and having her trust meant she could spend more time at Highlands. It would solve at least one of their problems. The thoughts of seeing her stirred his desire. Hopefully in solving one problem, he wasn't creating another.

His sister was right about one thing. He needed to watch himself when it came to Julia. As hard as it had been to get over her the first time, he might not survive another heartbreak.

One thing was certain, his return would stir up long-held questions of what he'd done that night in August and why his family suddenly left Magnolia Valley. Questions he couldn't answer and keep the promise he made to his parents. Questions he couldn't answer if he didn't want to see fear etched on Julia's face.

Chapter Five

Julia drove through the maze of lumber, bricks, and shingles then parked beside a dumpster that sat where a bronze fountain once had. She exited her car and gazed up at the hotel. Despite the patchwork of blue tarps covering the roof and plywood over many of the windows, progress had been made. Luke and his crew had ripped away the ruined siding and a new front door graced the entrance.

After opening her sedan's rear door, she approached a tradesman in the process of nailing molding to the column which supported the *porte-cochére*. "I brought you guys some lunch. If you could help—"

The guy in his late fifties dropped his hammer and was hefting the box of sandwiches from Grateful Bread before the words were hardly out of her mouth. "Thanks, Ms. Wilkes. This is great. Beats the hell—" He blushed and looked up at her. "—I mean, beats the heck out of the bologna and mustard sandwich I brought."

"You're very welcome. Thank you for doing such a good job on my building." She reached into the box for one of the orders. "Any chance Luke is here?" After chickening out during two other meetings, she'd made up her mind to broach the topic of their kiss.

His eyes widened. "Last time I saw him, he was

around back, reaming out the newbie, poor idiot that he is."

"Okay, thanks. Let me know how the guys like the sandwiches, and I'll go there again next week."

"Ms. Wilkes, you could bring us dog food and we'd be happy."

Julia rounded the corner to find Luke atop the scaffolding that wrapped around three sides of the building. Even from that height, his size made an impression with shoulders twice as big as most men and legs that went on forever. If it hadn't been for his distinctive eye color, she'd never recognized him for the young man with whom she'd fallen in love.

She cupped her hand to her mouth and called over the *rat-tat* of multiple nail guns. "Luke, can you come down here for a minute?"

As he looked down at her, his lips tightened. "I'm busy."

Great, so much for making things easy for me.

"It won't take but a minute." More than just his appearance had changed. In college, he'd been fun, easy going, and kind to the point of being gentle. None of those words applied to him, now. Anxiety twisted her stomach and her courage failed her. "I want to hear how the repairs are going."

He leapt from the scaffolding then stalked over to where she stood. "I told you to stay down at the barn. There's too many ways for you to get hurt up here."

Julia bristled at the scolding, but the desire to build a bridge over the unease running between them kept her tongue in check. "I brought the crew lunch." She held out the white bag to him.

"Thank you." He sat it on a nearby toolbox then

turned back to the scaffolding.

"I was hoping we could talk while you ate. I wanted to hear how things are going."

"Like I wrote in my email, we're a couple days ahead of schedule for the outside repairs and demo's begun on the inside."

She folded her arms across her chest. "I wanted to see things for myself." More to the point, she wanted to see if he'd do more than growl at her. "I'll be inside. I need to get a couple things out of my office."

He opened his mouth, but she cut him off. "I know, wear a hardhat and watch where you're walking." She might have many characteristics that made people think she was delicate, her slender figure for one and her fondness of pastel colors. That didn't mean she was careless. "I have to get the rest of my personal items out of my suite." Although where she was going to put them was still in question.

She had an appointment with a realtor to look at two houses to rent. Now that Teresa would be joining them, the pool of houses would be even more limited. Once inside her suite, she grabbed a couple suitcases from the closet and began collecting more clothes and Aiden's toys.

Julia held the plastic horses her son loved so much. Dogs were his favorite—real, stuffed, or cartoon, he loved them all. Horses were giving the canines a run for their money. Her heart ached recalling the conversation she'd had when she explained Aiden's favorite thing on the planet was no more. She couldn't say for certain the little boy understood, having never experienced death before.

Once Julia collected as much as she could, she

rolled the bags outside her rooms.

Luke stood waiting. "I've been meaning to discuss something with you." He took the bags and fell in step beside her.

Her heart sputtered. "Okay, sure." Would he finally address the elephant that had wedged its fat self between them? As they walked in silence, she braced for him to tell her the kiss had meant nothing, that he'd simply been comforting her.

When they reached her car, he loaded the bag into the back. "I have a proposition I want to run by you."

"Okay." Her shoulders sagged.

"You should bring your horses over to my stables. It's not safe to have them in the pasture, and your barn needs to be torn down."

"Really?" Tears stung her eyes. "You'd do that for me?" The small paddock was no place to keep her horses' long term, and she worried one of them would become injured in the pasture. His offer might not be a declaration of rekindled love, but it wasn't another rejection either.

On impulse, she threw her arms around him. "This is such a big relief."

"It's nothing really." Luke stiffened in her embrace. "No sense in mine standing empty."

She released her hold on him. "Sorry." She should have been more cognizant of his body language. Although he hadn't been like that before, clearly, he now hated physical contact.

"It's okay." He toed the ground with his boot. "It's been a long time since anyone touched me. My appearance tends to keep folks away."

Julia ached to soothe the pain he so fiercely

guarded. It wasn't his height or breadth that made people hesitant to take him on. It wasn't even the piercings and tattoos. They were simply the warning signs of the darkness emanating from his soul.

Perhaps, they were the armor he wore in the same way she used her designer wardrobe to give her the confidence she rarely felt. She leaned in and whispered, "I think that's what you *want* people to feel."

The corner of his mouth twitched. "Maybe."

She returned his smile. "You don't fool me. You're still a nice person underneath all that menace."

In an instant, the mask was back on. "Don't let that get out. I'll never get any work out of these guys."

"Your secret's safe with me." She savored the small victory, even as she reached for more. "Would it be okay if we rode over to your farm?"

Luke shifted his weight from foot to foot. "I guess. It's the same as it was; twenty stalls, tack room, and apartment above. I don't mind you taking a look-see. Give me five minutes, and we can head over."

She glanced over at his motorcycle parked next to a large white tent being used as a staging area for supplies. The image of her holding on to his waist, her thighs wrapped around his hips, flooded her brain. Her body heated. "That'd be great. I'll put my things in the car and be ready when you are."

Before she could suggest they use his bike, a luxury car pulled in, and Richard got out. Her pulse sped up. "I'll be right back. Let me see what he needs." She crossed the parking lot as fast as her boots would take her. "What's wrong?"

He offered her a too-perfect smile. "Does something have to be wrong for me to come see you?"

Julia forced breath into her lungs. In addition to cutting a path of destruction through North Georgia, the tornado had triggered her anxiety. She spent her days in fight-or-flight mode, waiting for the next catastrophic shoe to drop. "For you to risk your car's undercarriage, I imagine quite a lot must be wrong."

She and Richard had tabled the expansion plans until Highlands reopened. Despite the setback, she was more determined than ever to make her vision a reality. Was he looking for a way to gently back out of investing in her business?

"I called, and when you didn't answer, I took a chance I'd find you here. I want to treat you to lunch."

"I'm not dressed for anything back in Atlanta."

His gaze traveled over her. "You're perfect just as you are, but we can eat here in town if you'd rather."

Frustration simmered inside her. She didn't have time or the patience to untangle his subtext. In their early meetings, he'd been straightforward and businesslike. The switch in tack had her on the defensive. "I'm busy."

He cocked an eyebrow. "Too busy to discuss Wolfe Winery? I just came from a meeting with Topher Sutton and wanted to bring you up to speed."

Her pulse thrummed in her ears as her temper rose. "You went without me?"

"I know you've got your hands full with reconstruction, so I thought I'd take a couple things off your plate." He gestured to his car. "If you'll give me a chance, I'll tell you everything."

Julia reined in her attitude. In her zeal for independence, she forgot she didn't always need to shoulder every burden alone. "I'm sorry. Accepting help doesn't come easy for me. Give me a moment to clean up, and we'll go." On her way, she walked to where Luke was working. "I need to take a meeting with Richard. Can we still ride over to your place when I get back?"

He shrugged. "I'll be here."

She narrowed her gaze. His face was an unreadable mask, and yet she had the unmistakable feeling she'd upset him, that she'd somehow let him down. "I appreciate everything you're doing for me."

"It's no big deal, princess."

"It is to me." She touched his arm but when he tensed, she quickly withdrew it. "Sorry." His pained look tore at her heart. What had happened to him to make him hate human contact? She lowered her gaze. Maybe it was only her touch he despised. "I'll be back in an hour." She turned away from him before she could do anything else stupid like throwing her arms around him.

After washing the dust off her face and running a comb through her hair, she slid into Richard's car. "There's a place in town that has fast service." As she settled into the buttery soft seats, a sigh escaped her lips. "I need to be back as soon as possible."

Richard's lip curled as if he'd smelled something unpleasant. "I'm rather a gastronomic snob, I'm afraid. What's the name of this eatery with the expedient cuisine?"

Prior to purchasing her resort, she'd only known this part of Atlanta's ever-expanding suburbs as the town she'd passed through on her way to Rockaway Farm. Over the past three years, she'd come to appreciate Magnolia Valley's charm. "Don't worry.

Peggy's Diner has a fabulous lunch menu. It might not be as posh as Icehouse, but they serve a chicken salad to die for."

"Promise?" He flashed a grin before turning his attention to her driveway. He gripped the steering wheel and stared out the windshield until they reached the main highway. "Finally." He let out a breath. "I have to admit a certain amount of concern regarding the damage nails and debris might cause to my tires. Now, tell me, where is this illustrious eatery located?"

"On Main Street, just past the square." She stifled a yawn. Though she was used to working eighteen-hour days, the added stress was wearing her out. "It's the one with the bright pink awning." Her eyelids grew heavy. "Can't miss…"

Richard's hand brushed her cheek. "We're here, sleeping beauty."

Julia stretched, feeling refreshed from the catnap. "Sorry about that."

"How many hours are you putting in each day?" He leaned over to unfasten her seatbelt.

"No more than you, I expect." She reached for the door handle, letting herself out.

Richard bolted out of his side, meeting her on the sidewalk in front of the diner. His hand went to the small of her back as she led the way inside.

The proprietary gesture sent a fissure of unease dancing up her spine, and she had to resist the urge to brush his hand away. Instead, she quickened her steps as she located a booth at the far end of the long and narrow space.

After the waitress took their drink orders, Julia got to the matter at hand. "What did Topher Sutton have to say? Is he still interested in selling?"

Wolfe Winery sustained minor damage to the tank room since the tornado hopscotched over the area, but the barrel cellar and vineyard had been spared. As much as she hated the havoc the storm caused to her world, her situation could have been much worse. Several neighborhoods in the area had been wiped clean and a total of fourteen people died that day.

"We can talk about that in a moment." He leaned in, closing the distance between them. "First, how are you doing?"

"The insurance paid out, and the contractor is on schedule and within budget. I had to cancel all our events for April and May, but we should be open by the second weekend in June." Though she wasn't sure if she'd have any staff left. Many of those she'd laid off found jobs elsewhere.

Richard took her hand. "I'm not interested in the state of your business at this moment. I want to know how you're bearing up."

She snatched her hand away. "I'm fine." She sat a little straighter in her seat and ran a hand over her hair.

If he was offended by her actions, he didn't show it. "That's good to hear. I worry about you."

Did he think she wasn't up to the challenge? "There's nothing to concern you. I'm committed to my original expansion plans despite the setback. If you were able to allay any of Topher's concerns about Highlands reopening, I don't see why we can't move ahead."

"You don't have to do this you know."

"Do what?" She wasn't following his train of thought. "Purchasing Wolfe Winery is central to my plans. I want to make Highlands a real vacation destination for the region, a little slice of France tucked away in North Georgia."

His gaze bore into hers. "That's not what I am referring to. You don't have to struggle like this. There's another option, take the insurance money and walk away."

Her mouth gaped. "That never even crossed my mind. I've poured my heart and soul into Highlands. Even if I wasn't emotionally invested in the place, the little bit the insurance company paid me wouldn't last more than a year or two."

Especially given the repairs Oakton needed.

"I'm saying this as a friend." His smile widened. "I hope you consider me a friend."

"Sure," she managed, as she tried following the unexpected turn in their conversation. "I suppose you could say we're friends."

"Good, because I want you to know I'm here for you. I hope you'll consider me a shoulder to lean on."

Why did it sound like he was attempting to talk her out of the expansion plans? "I'll bare that in mind." She turned her attention to the Caesar salad. The leaves tasted like a scouring pad, though that was hardly Peggy's fault. Julia's stomach rolled as she tried to process the unexpected turn in their conversation.

Richard brought a bite of chicken salad to his mouth and chewed. Nodding, he said, "Your accolades weren't an exaggeration. This is excellent." He took several more bites and sipped some sweet tea before speaking again. "I should probably come to the point of my visit. I initiated the meeting with Mr. Sutton to ascertain if he planned to file a claim against you for his injuries."

Her eyes widened. "And?"

"Thankfully, no. He's recovering nicely and will entertain an offer for the purchase of his winery from you at some future date."

The tightness in her chest eased. "Wonderful." She stabbed her lettuce with a little more gusto, finishing her first meal since the tornado. The good news didn't, however, settle the mixed signals emanating from her investor.

Or are they mixed, after all?

His subtext-laced conversation, his body language, the unnecessary contact with Topher suggested he'd be happy to invest in more than her business.

After the meal ended and he'd driven her back to the hotel, she extended her hand. "Thank you for lunch. I'm glad to hear we're still making progress toward my expansion goal."

He took the hand she offered, bringing her fingers to his lips. "I hope you'll keep what I said in mind. I'm ready and willing to share your burden any time you wish."

"Certainly."

He then climbed in his car and drove off, leaving Julia staring at its taillights. She had been admired for her looks all her life, and she'd drawn the attention of the opposite sex from an early age, so Richard's not-so-subtle hints weren't unfamiliar. They weren't reciprocated, however.

And the man never far from her thoughts didn't want her.

She rounded the corner of the building, finding Luke beneath the staging tent. "Is now a good time to head to your place?"

He looked over his shoulder to his crew. "As good as any."

Julia took a couple steps toward his bike, anticipating the feel of the wind over her skin and Luke's body against hers. "Do you have a spare helmet?"

"We should take your car."

"Of course." Embarrassment heated her cheeks. "I don't know what I was thinking." She double-clicked her key fob to unlock the passenger door for him.

He folded himself into the sedan, sliding the seat as far back as it would go before he could fit his legs inside. "How was your lunch with Richie Rich?"

She chuckled. "Close. His name is Richard Pierce, and he's the venture capitalist who came to see Highlands the day of the storm. For now, he's holding off his investment until I can show him the repairs will be done as planned." Her arm brushed his as she put the car in gear. "Sorry."

"No problem." He moved his arm. "Don't worry about the schedule, either. I'm on time and under budget."

Her gaze jerked from the road ahead to him. "I have a mile-long list of things causing me nightmares, but you keeping your word isn't one of them."

"You're going to get through this, princess. You're tougher than you give yourself credit for."

She blossomed with his praise. "I am, aren't I?"

They turned off the main road, onto a gravel drive. Suddenly she wasn't the harried businesswoman. A dozen years rewound. Her heart sped up and tears formed in her eyes, not just because of the beauty of the fresh meadow on either side of the drive, but because she'd spent the happiest days of her life there. After the Chevaliers abruptly sold the farm, she never expected to see Rockaway Farm again. They crested a hill and the stone and timber house came into view.

"Nothing's changed." She parked in front of the house, and they both exited the car.

"I keep expecting my mother to come onto the porch and tell me dinner's ready."

She'd been fond of Pierre and Marie Chevalier. They'd been down-to-earth, welcoming to all who boarded at their farm, and a loving couple. "How are your parents doing? Will they be returning to Rockaway with you?"

"No." The light went out of his eyes. "They're dead."

"I'm sorry for your loss." A platitude that fell short at offering solace for the wounds etched on his face.

Luke drew her attention to the barn. "As you can see, your horses will have plenty of room. You're free to move your tack over as well."

"I don't know when I'll get the time to ride, but thanks."

"The fence is sound. I walked it the other day just to make sure."

"I can't thank you enough. Having a place for my horses is a huge weight off my mind."

"It's nothing, princess. No sense in letting all this room go to waste."

"I'd better head back. I'm meeting a realtor again today. I'm trying to find a place to rent."

"Where have you been staying?"

"Magnolia Valley Inn down by the highway."

"I figured you had a house in Atlanta."

"I did, but I sold it. Paul and I share custody, so Aiden has been staying with his father, but that's not a good long-term solution. My mother's home is also heavily damaged."

"So now the three of you need a place to live?"

"There are four of us actually. My former mother-in-law will be joining us. She's been staying at Paul's, but that's not working well." She waved a hand. None of this was his problem. "Anyway, I have to find a four-bedroom house that's near I-85 and is accessible for my mother with a broken leg."

"Stay here."

"What? No. I'm sorry, I wasn't hinting." She cringed at the thought. "Just talking out loud. You're already doing so much to help. I don't mean to complain."

"I know you weren't asking for help, but I want to do this."

"I can't displace you."

"I can stay in the apartment above the garage. It's got a bath and kitchenette."

She remembered the space well. They'd used it as their getaway place. What would it be like to come home to him each night? To have him near. Would he hide from her as he did at the resort? "I accept your gracious offer."

Could this lead to other wonderful things?

Chapter Six

Back at Highlands, Julia ran her hand along Misty's swollen flank. Maybe it was her imagination, but she thought a tiny hoof nudged her hand through the mare's belly. "You're going to be such a good mama," Julia cooed, hoping to soothe the horse's nerves. "Much better than I was at first."

Julia and Paul hadn't planned to start a family when she learned she was pregnant. His business was becoming a success, and he was working nearly round the clock to see that it stayed that way. They'd bought a big house, and when she wasn't busy decorating the five-thousand square foot Tutor mansion, she was riding or having her nails done.

Expanding out of her designer clothes, babies, bottles, and diapers weren't in her plans. She fought her new reality.

Something close to a miracle had happened about six months after Aiden's birth. It was as if her maternal instincts needed a kick start. She fired the nanny and started being a real mother to her little boy.

Unfortunately, the change came too late to save her marriage. After Aiden's birth, Julia had an affair. It had been brief and meaningless but catastrophic, nonetheless. Paul found out and though he'd stayed, he hadn't been able to forgive her. She'd been the one to initiate the divorce, believing he deserved a second chance at love. Thankfully, he'd gotten that with Michelle.

Maybe she would as well one day. Richard's thinly veiled offer echoed in her ear. From a distance, they made a good match—her breeding and family name paired with his money to create a new dynasty. Nothing about him came near to the desire Luke inspired, not even a little spark ignited. In her world, where marriage could be more merger than love match, sexual passion wasn't a necessity for marriage. However, it was essential for her.

With Luke, perhaps?

Not likely considering it took two willing participants to build a life together. Each conversation they shared only confirmed at best he merely tolerated her. While her love for him deepened with each passing day.

"Men are complicated creatures, aren't they?"

Misty shifted her weight, leaning into Julia's body. "That's it; take a load off, girl." She kept up with the brushing. Her horses had had a rough life before they got to her and the tornado escalated their anxiety. The whole herd had been on edge since the storm. Yesterday, Lady, a Shetland pony, bit her bestie, Daisy, and Sookie, a Quarter Horse mix, started cribbing, the nervous habit of chewing on the stall.

From down the way, D'Artagnan let out a high pitched whiny that sounded suspiciously like a command.

"I'll get to you in a minute. Ladies first."

Today was moving day for her herd. Joe-Lee would be there later that afternoon to relocate them to Luke's farm which is why she had everyone stabled.

She opened the door to D'Artagnan's stall and scooted through the opening before closing the door behind her. "You and I need to have a serious conversation." She nudged him out of the way to drop a scoop of grain into his bucket. "We're all moving over to Luke's farm today, which is going to be so much better than here." She scratched underneath the horse's forelock, his favorite spot. "You know Luke. He's the man who brings you carrots."

D'Artagnan bumped Julia's shoulder. "You and your sweet tooth." She opened her palm so the horse could get at the lump of sugar. "I need this to make you a little sweeter."

Julia recalled the day her boy arrived at Highlands. He practically kicked his way out of the trailer, injuring his handler in the process. She'd wanted to have horseback riding as an amenity for her guests as well as pleasure riding for her and Aiden. Seeing D'Artagnan snort and buck around the paddock had her second guessing her decision. It took her weeks to get near the animal and months of coaxing to finally get a saddle on him.

They'd made friends in the process, with him finally learning to trust his new mistress. Climbing onto his back and having him stand perfectly still was one of her proudest moments. She'd turned a fearful animal that had reason to be distrustful of humans into a lamb, for her at least. He shied away from visitors to the barn, retreating to the back of his stall when Rachel came to ride. He actively hated men. Her boy bit and kicked any other male that came near, so for obvious reasons she'd left instructions with Joe-Lee to leave D'Artagnan for her to trailer.

The sound of a car along the drive brought everyone's head up. Julia peeked out the window at the back of the stall in time to see Rachel's car pass. She'd asked her friend to come up for a few hours to help her inventory usable equipment and furniture. Highlands was a long way from reopening, but she needed to submit purchase orders now. She still held out hope she'd also be planning an upgrade to the furnishings and a redesign of the golf course.

As she slipped out of the stall, D'Artagnan called after her.

"I'll be back in a little while. You be good."

Catching up to Rachel, she gave the woman a hug. "Thank you for coming to help."

"Glad to do it." She followed Julia around the back of the building to the construction entrance. "I'm bored just hanging around my place." She caught Julia's eyes as they reached one of the undamaged ballrooms used for storing the salvaged furniture. "Speaking of houses, did you ever find a place to rent?"

"I didn't tell you?" Her stomach gave a flutter as she thought about how close she'd be to him. "Luke offered me his place."

Rachel's eyes widened. "Luke, the contractor, Luke? You're moving in with him?"

"Not moving in with him." Her voice climbed an octave. "He's going to be staying in an apartment over his stable. Mother, Aiden, Teresa, and I are going to live in his house." That proximity would be enough to keep her rattled.

"Wow." She sank into a club chair that had been rescued from the lounge on the second floor. "I don't know what shocks me more, that you're taking your former mother-in-law with you or that beast of a man is doing more than growling at someone."

Julia picked up the nearby clipboard she'd prepared for doing inventory and began flipping through the attached pages. "He's not that bad. Beneath all the gruffness, he's a nice guy."

Rachel moved a few paces away and began counting the folding chairs leaning against one wall. "That's a huge assumption on your part. I don't think you know him as well as you think you do."

"I told you, we used to be friends."

"Which I still find hard to believe." Rachel met Julia's gaze. "There's something up with him."

The understatement of the decade.

"You're just reacting to the tattoos and piercings." And probably his scowl, too.

Every time she saw him, it took her a moment to resolve the change with how he'd looked as a younger man.

"No. I've been around guys like that when I worked in a gym in Atlanta. He gives off some seriously dark vibes."

Luke wouldn't hurt anyone. Beneath the course exterior lay the gentle man she'd once known. Julia waved away her concern. "Don't let the skull-trim and leather jacket scare you."

Rachel stopped her work and turned her full attention to the conversation. "That's not what has me bothered. It's the way he follows you with his eyes when you're around that worries me."

"He watches me?"

"All the time. It's like he's guarding you or something."

"I hadn't noticed." It seemed like he was trying to avoid her, not keep tabs.

"Just be careful, okay." Rachel's brow furrowed with concern. "He's not the man you think he is."

Julia might not know the reason why his family left Magnolia Valley or how he'd spent the past twelve years, but beneath the rough exterior laid the man she remembered. "If he's so awful," she began, feeling a bit defensive both of Luke and her judgement. "Why is he letting me move into his house?"

Rachel's gaze bore into hers. "I think that's a question you need to answer for yourself before you move your family in with him."

"I have." Pity and the need to rescue had something to do with the offer, of that much she was certain. Did he share her attraction? Was keeping her close part of his motivation for helping her? "I've thought of little else." She pushed the lingering questions to the side in favor of the work at hand.

A couple hours later, the furniture-filled room had been organized and catalogued.

"How's Brad doing? Any word when the dealership might reopen?" Julia asked, as they treated themselves to a much-deserved break.

Rachel shook her head. "No idea." She took a sip from her soft drink. "But he's got a job interview somewhere else."

"Oh, my goodness. That's so great. Please tell me it's something with a steady salary."

After Rachel's husband got out of the army, he could only find employment selling used cars on commission. "It is," she said, relief evident in her voice.

"Tell me about it."

“It’s a teaching position at Swainsboro Military School.”

Julia kept her face neutral. She couldn’t resent her friend’s good fortune even if it meant she would be hundreds of miles away. “I’ll keep my fingers crossed that he gets it.”

“I’m trying not to get my hopes up, but I’ll keep you posted if we hear anything.”

“I think we’re done for the day. Thanks for your help.” She let out a breath as she surveyed the work they’d done. “This would have taken me days to do alone.”

“Let me know if you need me again.” Rachel collected her purse off a nearby table.

Julia led the way through halls filled with scaffolding, wondering how her other employees were getting on. “I’m sorry about having to lay off everyone.”

Rachel stopped with her hand on the push bar. “The tornado wasn’t your fault.”

No, but that didn’t assuage her guilt. She looked around the rear of the hotel, to the pool and now unkempt landscape. A sense of urgency tightened her chest.

As they made their way to the front, Julia’s gaze darted to the barn. She spotted the huge trailer. “Darn, when did Joe-Lee get here? They weren’t due for another couple hours.” She said her goodbyes to Rachel and headed down to the barn.

A heavy rain had fallen the night before, making the ground a soggy mess. As she neared the large trailer, parked some distance from the barn, she noted most everyone had been loaded. A young man came out of the barn leading Misty toward the trailer. “Everything going well?” she asked him as she gave the horse a pat.

“Nearly done. Joe-Lee’s getting ready to bring out another horses.”

Julia increased her pace, not wanting to keep her barn manager waiting while she loaded D’Artagnan.

“Get the fuck away from that animal.” Luke’s angry voice added speed to her steps.

“I know what I’m doing.”

Joe-Lee? What were he and Luke arguing about?

“Like hell you do.”

The crack of a whip snapped through the air. D’Artagnan’s roar followed. Her legs couldn’t carry her fast enough. The horse’s screams pierced the air.

The sudden stop chilled her to the core.

What had Joe-Lee done to her horse?

Tears blurred her vision as she raced toward the barn.

D’Artagnan burst out of the barn, trailing his lead line behind him. She would have chased after him, but at that speed Mercury would have had a tough time catching up. Safe inside the pasture, the stallion could calm down while she dealt with his tormentor.

The silence shifted to the sounds of a scuffle. A fist meeting flesh. She raced into the barn to find Luke pummeling Joe-Lee. Repeatedly his clenched hands met the guy’s body. Blood flowed down Joe-Lee’s face and soaked his shirt.

“Luke, stop!” she screamed. “Stop! You’re hurting him.”

He kept up the beating as if she’d never spoken. Backing D’Artagnan’s tormentor against a stall, Luke lifted Joe-Lee by the neck. "Teach you to hit an animal."

Julia clung to Luke's arm trying to pry him off. "Stop it. Luke, stop it now."

He froze.

Joe-Lee fell to the sawdust floor.

Luke's breath came in pants. "He was hurting your horse. Drawing blood." He trained his attention on the man at his feet. "Get. Out. Of. *Here*!" His roar reverberated through the empty barn.

Joe-Lee swiped at the blood on his face with his shirt tail. "Gladly." He turned to Julia. "You can haul your own goddamned animals. Too bad only that little shit pony died in the tornado. Should have been all of them."

Julia lunged for the guy, ready to finish what Luke started. However, Joe-Lee sidestepped her and lit out of the barn nearly as fast as D'Artagnan.

"How can I ever thank—" She turned to find Luke had taken Joe-Lee's place in the sawdust. "What's wrong?"

He buried his head in his hands. "God, I really lost it. That hasn't happened to me in years."

Julia knelt beside him. "You saved my horse. Joe-Lee was hurting him." She wrapped her arm around him. "Thank you. It looks like I owe you again."

"It's me who's in your debt." He let out a shuttering breath. "I would have killed that man."

She took his face in her palms. "He deserved what he got. I only wish I could have been the one to give him a taste of his own abuse." She envied him for his strength, for his ability to protect others. All she'd been able to do was let down those she loved.

He looked up at her, his eyes anguished and vacant. “Violence solves nothing. It’s a temporary fix with forever consequences.”

“Of course.” Julia attempted to make sense of Luke’s words considering what she’d just witnessed. She took his hand, shocked when he allowed the contact. “But you protected D’Artagnan.”

“Terrible consequences,” he muttered as if she wasn’t there.

A chill ran through her. Was violence at the root of why his family sold their farm and disappeared?

Chapter Seven

The next day, Luke took the apartment stairs down to the tack room and then into the center aisle of the barn. He'd moved from the house in preparation for Julia and her family who were arriving later that day. "Figures the day I need to be early to the job site, I oversleep." Usually five or six hours were enough for him, but last night he'd put in a full eight horizontal hours.

Several of Julia's horses stuck their noses out to greet him. "Good morning, everybody." He stretched to get the blood flowing to his muscles. "How'd you sleep?"

All night, they called to each other, softly nickering back and forth, still getting accustomed to their new home. Maybe the lullaby of his early years was the reason he'd rested so well. Misty called to him, as eager for human interaction as a yellow lab he'd once had. "Okay, since I'm already late." He backtracked to the feed room for a scoop of oats. As he stepped inside to pour the grain in her trough, she nudged his shoulder. "You're welcome, little mama. That should do you until Julia gets here."

She'd be there later and wanted to be the one to let the horses out into their new pasture. He'd assured her the fence was sound, but she'd wanted to be nearby in case one decided to go walkabout. She was also handling the move of her furniture. What had he been thinking when he'd made the offer? He was supposed to be keeping his distance from the beautiful woman, not moving her into his family's home.

Luke worked his way down the length of the barn, checking to see how the horses had passed their first night. He'd fallen into old patterns as if the last dozen years had never existed. After the incident with the horse transport, Julia hadn't been willing to risk her herd to anyone else. The two of them had hauled them over in the two-horse trailer she owned. Everything had gone smoothly until it came to loading D'Artagnan. Luke had been anxious to help, but as it was he'd been more of a hindrance. The stallion couldn't abide anyone but his mistress.

Luke could hardly blame the horse. He'd happened by the barn when he first heard the abuse. No living creature, human or animal, deserved the whipping D'Artagnan received. Even if he was stubbornness personified.

"Speaking of the devil." Luke reached the lone male's stall. "How're your lashes doing?" He noted the marks left by the barn manager seemed to be healing thanks to the ointment Julia applied. His brow furrowed seeing the animal hadn't eaten a thing. "You feeling alright?" Caring for the animals came as natural as looking after Julia did. Luke unlatched the stall door and stepped inside, so he could check the horse's belly. The last thing she needed was to lose the stallion to colic. D'Artagnan backed his ears and tossed his head.

"It's alright," Luke cooed. "Just want to take a quick look."

Being in an enclosed space was dangerous, most

especially when the animal didn't want him there. Over the years, he'd been kicked and bitten a few times, but had managed to escape without any serious injuries. The horse gave a loud snort. From the sound of things, this one wanted to change that record.

Luke inched forward, speaking softly to the frightened animal. When he finally got near enough, he ran his hand over the horse's flank. Using a stethoscope to check for bowel sounds would have been better, but he hadn't owned one of those in years. The rumblings felt normal, but the animal bore watching. "I'll let Julia know you're off your feed this morning." He backed toward the door.

Quicker than Luke could outmaneuver, D'Artagnan leaned out. "Shit!" Luke hissed as the horse bit his forearm. He clamped a hand over the bite. "Three Musketeers my ass, she should have named you Satan."

The horse tossed his head and snorted as if he agreed. If Luke hadn't seen for himself the one-eighty shift the horse made when Julia was around, he would have worried for her safety. She brought out the horse's better nature. "Looks like we have a lot in common," he said begrudgingly admitting the woman coaxed from him emotions buried beneath years of hurt and layers of hate. He shook his head to loosen himself from reflection.

Luke retreated upstairs for the first aid kit. He touched his red and swollen arm. "Dang, that animal got me a good one." Bruises highlighted the distinct imprint of D'Artagnan's teeth. "At least he didn't break the skin."

After strapping on a bag of frozen peas, he headed

over to Highlands. He was late by a good half hour and took some ribbing from his crew. A couple days of rain put them behind schedule, so he set aside the paperwork that usually kept him busy and spent the morning working alongside the guys.

As the day passed, he found his thoughts straying to Julia. His ears straining for the sound of her car. His heart beating double time. He wasn't the only one having difficulty staying on track. "What are you looking for?" he asked the foreman spending more time watching the driveway than nailing siding.

He shrugged. "Hoping the owner will pay us a visit."

One of the younger guys on his crew gave Doug a jab in the ribs. "You forget to pack your lunch?"

His face split into a grin. "Yeah, but that's not why. Damn, that woman is a looker."

Luke's blood heated, and he reminded himself that guys liked to talk. If they kept things polite, he'd let them.

"I think I'll mark some time with her." Pete ran his fingers through his hair.

Doug barked a laugh. "Like she'd give you the time of day."

"Too good for you, too."

"I heard that."

Luke would do well to remember their words. Julia had been born into a class of Atlanta society no amount of money could elevate him to. She'd only grown better over the years, becoming more ethereal, if that were possible. While he'd become grittier. Five years in prison would do that to a man. He'd changed to survive in that environment, and the loss of his true self angered him as much as the loss of time. "Stop yammering you two. Get to work or I'm docking your pay."

Luke drove his crew until it was too dark to swing a hammer. Catching up due to the bad weather wasn't his only reason for putting in the long hours. He'd put off returning to the farm as long as possible. Didn't trust himself to be alone with Julia. That kiss hadn't been nearly enough. He craved the touch of her lips the way a drunk craved whiskey.

The clawing need kicked up a notch as he pulled up in front of the house. He found Julia leaning her head against the back of his mom's swing as she pushed against the porch with her foot. Even from that distance, he could tell she, too, had put in a hard day's work.

Leave her alone. Turn away.

His feet had other ideas. He was off the bike and headed her way, cursing himself with each step. "How'd it go today?"

"Good. I've still got a lot of unpacking to do, but everything's moved in." Fatigue laced each word.

"Need some help?"

"I've got it." As she stretched, the hem of her T-shirt rode up, revealing a too-slender waist. "I managed to convince my mother we wouldn't be entertaining much while we're here, so she's kept things to a minimum."

"Have you eaten recently?" He recalled she'd battled an eating disorder as a teen.

She waved away his concern, just as she'd done all those years ago. "I'm fine."

"You need to eat." He was only riding her for her own good. "Come up to the apartment. I'll make us some dinner."

She wrinkled up her face. "No, no, no. I'm a sweaty mess."

"Like I've been swimming in cologne all day." He gestured to the front door as the need to care for her took hold. "Get cleaned up and come over. You need to eat."

A small smile played at her lips. "You're awfully bossy tonight."

"More than usual?" He cocked an eyebrow at the accusation he'd heard all his life.

"No, the same. Okay. I'll be over as soon as I take a shower." She stood then walked the few steps to the front door. "Should I bring anything? I think there's a bottle of wine in one of the boxes."

He shifted from foot to foot, suddenly rethinking his plan. He'd meant only to get some food inside her, not ask her on a date. "Yeah, that'd be great." Maybe wine would help take the edge off. He headed for the barn.

"Luke."

His name on her lips stopped him as surely as if she had a lasso around his neck. "Yeah, princess?"

"Thanks."

"It's just food," he said it as much for his benefit as hers. "Everybody's got to eat."

She shook her head. "Not about that."

Irritation bubbled inside him. He didn't want her to be grateful or feel obligated to him. He turned to face her. "Enough," he barked. "Stop thanking me every time I turn around."

She took a step back then lowered her gaze. "Sorry. I just wanted you to know I appreciate everything you've done for me."

He clenched his fists. Dammit, why did she have to be so beautiful? Why did he want to be a better man, so he might come somewhere in the neighborhood of deserving her? "I haven't done anything special, nothing some other person wouldn't do for you." Hell, men would stand in line to play Prince Charming to her Distressed Damsel. "So, stop thanking me for being human."

Julia tilted her chin. "Just forget about dinner. I'm not hungry anyway."

He dropped his head to his chest and let out a breath. "Ignore me, okay. I haven't done much socializing in the past few years, and I guess I've forgotten how to be nice."

"I'll say." She peeked up at him and smiled. "You sound a lot like Brad."

"Who's he?"

"Rachel's husband. When he first came back from Afghanistan, he was like a wounded bear. Rachel changed all that."

He closed the distance to tower over her. She needed to get one thing clear. "This is me now. I've changed. Permanently. Take it or leave it."

She met his gaze. "Whatever you say. I'll see you after I shower."

God, he didn't need that image in his brain.

"Fine. Do what you want." He turned on his heels and fled to his apartment before he acted on his body's urging.

****

Luke spent the next half hour putting together dinner and attempting to get a handle on his lust. At the soft rap on his door, he let her in, only to have Little Luke ignore all his admonitions. She'd braided her wet hair and smelled of fabric softener.

Her gaze scanned the room. "It hasn't changed, either. I swear it's like stepping back in time." She moved to the room's lone window. "I used to sneak up here." She turned to him. "Even when we weren't together. I'd stare down at your house and wonder what it would be like to live in it."

"Why would you do that?" He loved this family home, but it was nothing compared to the mansion she grew up in.

She turned her back on him. "Just did."

He could count each vertebra through her T-shirt. "Come, let's eat." He'd made a salad, thinking he might get her to eat that.

Julia took the seat across from him. "This looks lovely. You didn't have to go to so much trouble."

Seeing her in his space shouldn't have made him so pleased. He shrugged. "No trouble. Everybody's got to eat, even you." He uncorked the Riesling she brought and poured each of them a glass.

Julia drained hers in a couple long draws then refilled her glass—all the while chasing lettuce around her plate.

"Something wrong with the food?"

"No." She popped a strawberry in her mouth. "It's delicious. I just have a lot on my mind."

"Want to tell me about it? I'm a good listener."

"Not especially." She pointed to his arm. "Want to tell me how you got that bite?"

He chuckled. "I'll tell if you will."

The corner of her mouth turned up. "You first."

She drained the second glass.

"I was checking on the horses this morning and D'Artagnan took exception to my examining him."

"I bet he did. Sometimes I wonder why I bought him."

"I wondered that myself. He hates the world and everyone in it. Clearly, he's had a hard start to life."

"I guess that's what drew me to him. I thought I could make things better. Gentle out the rough spots. Show him not everyone was out to hurt him."

If she thought she could do the same to him, she was wrong, dead wrong. No amount of gentle persuasion could change the indelible mark prison made on him.

She took a bite of salad, chewed, and swallowed. "Exercise will calm him down. If things go well, I should be able to get over here a few times this week to ride him. I can't wait to take him for a run across your pasture."

"That should take the edge off. You probably know this already, but it bears mentioning anyway. Watch everyone for signs of colic over the next few days while they get used to the fresh grass."

As she reached across the table to take his hand, her expression warmed. "You're still so good with horses. What made you go into construction instead of opening up a practice?"

He'd been too long away from school when he'd gotten paroled. Other options in the field didn't appeal. He hadn't wanted to be reminded of all he'd lost. "Just didn't."

Her smile disappeared. "I should get back." She placed her napkin on the table and rose. "The moms are coming tomorrow, and I still have dozens of boxes to unpack."

Luke had her in his arms before his brain could weigh in on the impulse. His lips met hers. She mewled and opened for him. She tasted of strawberry and sweet wine. He meant to pull away. Needed to rein in his lust. Nothing good could come of them being together. Having her up in the space that held so many happy memories had been a mistake, one that would only lead to them both getting hurt. When her arms twined around his back, he lost all hope of stopping. Especially as her fingernails dug into his back.

He broke the kiss. "This shouldn't be happening."

She drew her T-shirt over her head. "Why not, if it's what we both want?"

The creamy swells of her breasts called to him. He cupped one, thumbing her nipple through the lace of her bra. There were dozens—hundreds even—of reasons why sex with Julia would only make things worse. None came to mind now.

"Make love to me, Luke." Her jeans hit the floor, revealing a pink lace thong on slender hips. "Make me forget what a train wreck my life is." She stood before him, baring both her body and soul to him.

He scooped her into his arms and stormed the few feet to his bed. After he'd laid her there, she loosened the band tying her hair and ran her fingers through it. The braid left her light-blonde hair wavy, and when she leaned back against the pillow it fanned out, making her look even more like a goddess than she already did.

Julia patted the mattress. "Come, lay down next to me."

His heart pounded against his chest. He toed off

his shoes. Shucked out of his jeans. "You don't know how many times I've thought about this." Twin desires warred inside him. He brushed a hand from her shoulder to her hip. "I want to savor…"

She cut off his words. "Next time."

Would there be a next time? Should there be? All he wanted in that moment was to make them both forget what lay beyond the walls of his apartment.

"Oh, Luke, I love you." She nuzzled closer.

He froze. Had he heard right?

"I love you so much."

"No, no, no." He leapt from the bed. "You can't say that."

"But I mean it."

"Take it back." He pulled on his jeans. "That's the wine talking. You can't possibly love me. You haven't seen me in years."

"But that doesn't matter." She reached for him. "I already loved you. I don't think I ever stopped. Seeing you again brought it all back. I tried to forget you, but I never did." Tears shimmered on her cheeks.

He scooped up her clothes and tossed them to her. "That is not what this is about. Get dressed."

She ducked her chin as she drew on the jeans and T-shirt.

"I won't take advantage of you." He reined in his emotions. "You've been through a lot in a very short period of time and are confusing lust with love."

"I'm sorry." Her words came as a whisper. "But it's how I feel."

"Look at me." When she refused to meet his gaze, he took her by the shoulders, careful not to hold her too tightly. "Then you need to get a serious grip on your feelings."

She struggled against his hold. "Let me go. I get it. You don't feel the same way."

Her tears shamed him. He couldn't do anything but hurt her. "It's not a matter of my feelings toward you. I simply can't act on them. Or at least I shouldn't. Find someone you can be proud of. Someone who can help you. Like—" The guy's name caught in this throat. He didn't deserve her either, but he came a lot closer to it than Luke did. "You should be with that Pierce guy."

"I'm not in love with him."

"You should try harder."

She brushed away tears. "I can't control who I fall in love with any more than I can control the weather."

"But we both can control how we act on those emotions. I'm the wrong guy for you despite my feelings. I hurt you once. I won't do it again."

This time when she struggled, he let her escape.

Chapter Eight

Sunday morning, Luke peered from the window overlooking the farmhouse. He imagined Julia seated at the kitchen table drinking coffee with the wallpaper roosters staring over her shoulder. Later, she'd wash breakfast dishes at his mother's sink then finish unpacking her possessions, placing them in rooms his loved ones once used.

He let the curtain fall. It did no good to visualize what he could never be a part of. Tidying as he paced the long, narrow apartment, he made quick work of the day's tasks. The hours until he could return to the jobsite stretched endlessly before him. He barked a bitter laugh. Twenty-four hours shouldn't seem like such an eternity compared to the years he'd served. Perhaps, he'd saddle one of Julia's horses and take it for a ride.

As he reached the tack room, a large sedan ambled up the driveway and parked in front of the house. Julia burst out of the front door, exchanged a few words with the driver, and then moved to the rear of the car to assist an older woman in a leg cast. Another late-middle aged lady and a trunk load of suitcases joined them.

Luke stood before one of the stalls, saddle in hand, envisioning the well-to-do women clucking around the living room, passing judgement on his mother's home. He shook his head. "Who cares what they think," he told Oreo, a black and white Quarter Horse. "As long as Julia and you girls are taken care of." D'Artagnan let out a whinny. "You, too, Satan's Little Helper."

After saddling the horse, he galloped her to the farthest part of his property. The two then explored a small creek to the north before visiting the east pasture. Several hours later, he walked a sweat-soaked mare into the barn. "Let's get you cooled down, girl. Then we'll have a good brushing and a couple carrots. How's that sound?"

"I often think horses make better company than people."

Luke stiffened as Julia drew near. His gaze darted to the apartment door, but a retreat wasn't possible. The horse required care after the strenuous ride, but more importantly, he wouldn't add to the hurt he'd already inflicted upon her. He picked up a brush from the bucket at his feet and began grooming the mare. "Getting the grand ladies settled?"

Her shoulders slumped. "As much as I can. It looks like they're going to be more of a challenge than my son. Frankly, I'm starting to think it was a mistake to bring them here."

His hand tightened on the brush. "The house not good enough for them?"

"It's not that. They wanted me to express their thanks for letting us take over your home." Her gaze latched on to his. "But I know how much you hate gratitude."

He despised himself for being the one to put the pain in her proud expression. "About that, I was out of line. I'm sorry."

"You're forgiven. However, extracting an apology

wasn't why I came out here. The moms want to extend an invitation to dinner this evening. I told them you were too busy, but they insisted I come out here and ask."

Bad idea. Refuse.

He'd probably give the ladies a heart attack. However, the opportunity to spend time with Julia proved too enticing. "I accept. What time should I come?"

Her eyes widened. "Seven o'clock."

"Does your family dress for dinner?"

"Usually, but tonight we'll be casual."

He winked. "Good thing. My tux is at the cleaners."

She backed away, surprise still evident on her face. "I'll see you then."

Promptly at the hour requested, Luke stood on his front porch dressed in his only pair of nice slacks, button-down shirt, and loafers. Following a knock, Julia admitted him into the living room. Her mother and former mother-in-law sat on armchairs flanking the fireplace. He bowed to them. "*Bonne soiree, dames. Merci pour ton invitation.*"

He braced for the two older women's reactions. No amount of showering, removal of piercings, or French could hide what years in prison had wrought. Ordinarily, he didn't bother putting people at ease. Either his size and appearance intimidated them, or it didn't. For Julia he'd made the effort. "I brought a Merlot from Wolfe Winery. I thought it would go nicely with dinner."

"That's perfect." Julia's smile lit up his chest and made all the pains he'd gone through worthwhile.

"Luke, please meet my former mother-in-law, Teresa Wilkes and my mother Helene Chandler." She took him by the hand and drew him closer. "Moms, I'd like you to meet Luke Chevalier, a friend of mine from many years ago."

"*Enchantee*." He bowed to each woman.

Mrs. Chandler narrowed her gaze. "*You're* our landlord?"

"Yes, I suppose I am, ma'am."

Julia stiffened. "Mother, you will recall Luke has very graciously moved to his apartment above the stables, so we'd have a comfortable place to live."

Teresa walked to the corner of the room where a small bar had been set up and poured two glasses of sherry. "What do you do for a living, Mr. Chevalier?"

He squared his shoulders, refusing to let anyone make him feel less than because he worked with his hands. His occupation allowed him to purchase the place they were calling home now. "I own a construction company, the one that's currently rebuilding Julia's resort."

"So, you see how hard she's working. Perhaps *you* can make our Julia see sense." She handed one glass to Helene before returning to her seat. "We think she should sell Highlands as soon as you make the necessary repairs."

"I'm afraid you won't find me an ally in that pursuit. I believe Julia can make her resort a success."

"But she works so hard," Mrs. Wilkes countered.

Julia clenched her fist. "Work is not a four-letter word, Teresa. It's what humans were designed to do."

Helene placed her glass on the table at her elbow with a thud strong enough to make the crystal sing. "I'll have you know, we've both contributed to our community. We just didn't kill ourselves in the process."

"I didn't mean to imply otherwise Mother." She massaged the bridge of her nose. "You've done a great deal for the arts in Atlanta. I simply meant my work is important to me."

A timer dinged in the kitchen, sending Julia to her feet. "That's dinner. Luke, will you escort the moms into the dining room while I bring in the food?"

"My pleasure."

Luke's mother would have approved of the changes Julia made to her humble dining room. The small area, which was open to both the kitchen and living room, was filled with a French country table, sideboard, and hutch. Armless chairs, upholstered in creamy linen, lined the oak table. Once he'd seated the two older women, he remained standing until Julia returned. After helping her with the dishes, he took the seat closest to her, sensing she needed an ally during the meal. The salad course passed with only the sound of cutlery against china to break the silence.

While they enjoyed her delicious roast, the moms brought up Julia's former charity work, her friends back in Atlanta, and an upcoming exhibit at the High Museum of Art. Julia's shoulders grew more taunt and her back more rigid as the women continued to make their opinions known.

"When will Aiden be joining you?" he asked to divert their attention.

Relief shown in her eyes. "Paul is bringing him up tomorrow. I can't wait to get my arms around him. Being away from him so much has been the most difficult part of this whole ordeal."

"I'm looking forward to meeting him."

"I'm sure you'll see him around the barn." She flashed a tense smile.

Had he assumed? Would she prefer he kept his distance? "Perhaps, we can save the formal introductions until he's had time to adjust to his new surroundings."

"That's one of the many worries on my mind, but I'm hoping seeing the horses will help with the transition."

Mrs. Chandler set down her wine glass and dabbed the corner of her mouth with a napkin. "Now that the pony is gone, I think it would be best if you redirected Aiden's attention. I don't think his obsession with horses is healthy."

"I agree," Mrs. Wilkes chimed in. "Perhaps art lessons would suit him better."

Every muscle in Julia's body stiffened as the women continued to tag-team her. Luke shared a portion of her frustration having spent the meal under their judgmental gaze. What else could he do short of carrying her out of the house?

"You ready to head out, Julia?" A plan took form as he stood from the table. "Ladies, it's been a pleasure."

Her brows knitted as she followed his queues. "Do you think I'll need a jacket?"

"Definitely." He pointed to her sandal-clad feet. "And closed-toe shoes."

While Julia scurried out of the room, he soothed the matron's ruffled feathers. "I promised Julia I'd take her out for ice cream." The thought of her body wrapped around him sent his imagination into overdrive. A thousand ways the plan could go south ran through his brain. However, the thrill of making Julia happy drowned out the harpies' shrill warning. "It's been a pleasure meeting you ladies." He kissed the top of each woman's hand. "Would you like us to bring you back something?"

****

Once they'd escaped their audience, Julia threw herself into Luke's arms. "You were brilliant back there. You had them eating out of your hand." She sobered. "I know I'm not supposed to say this anymore but thank you."

Her pulse thrummed as she followed him to his motorcycle. After last night, she hadn't expected to catch more than a glimpse of him, and certainly not have him accept her mother's invitation to dinner. She wouldn't have conjured up the bike-ride escape in a hundred years. Having been tightly pressed against his hard body the night before, she couldn't wait to put herself in that predicament again, even if it wasn't good for her. Or would lead to nothing.

He glared at her as if he already regretted his invitation. "Put this on." He thrust a helmet toward her. She climbed behind him and they took off screaming down the narrow drive leading to the main road.

Her arms around his narrow waist, legs around his hips, she settled in. His heat penetrated the light jacket she wore, giving her just the right amount of warmth to counter the cool evening air. She'd been such a fool to mess things up last night with her confession. Why hadn't she kept those three words to herself? It was clear as the sky above that he didn't feel the same way.

At one time he had loved her. Not only had he said it frequently, he'd shown it.

Could he love her again?

Julia forced her thoughts away from the hamster wheel of why, why, why. Right now, she was where she wanted to be, and though it was far from ideal she'd learned moments didn't have to be perfect to be appreciated. She clung to his body as they took the curves and turns. All too soon they arrived at their destination.

She took off her helmet, her heart still beating furiously from the ride. "That's the most fun I've had in years."

His gaze narrowed as she ran her fingers through her hair in a futile attempt to undo the effects of the helmet. "Well almost." She ducked her chin. She'd give her best pair of shoes to be naked with him again, even if it would end the same way. There was something addicting about the way his body fit against hers. That hadn't changed. He'd always moved with such sensuous grace it made her heart ache to watch him.

He took off his helmet and placed it on the seat beside her. "Wait over at the picnic table."

She did as he bid, her eyes following him as he crossed the parking lot to join the line waiting to order.

The things that man does to a pair of jeans.

It should have bothered her that he hadn't asked what she wanted. Not like it mattered. What she wanted wouldn't be found on the board above the window.

He returned a short time later with two dishes. After straddling the bench across from her, he slid one of them her way.

Vanilla. He remembered.

She stared at the creamy goodness melting in the spring air.

"Something wrong? You don't like vanilla anymore?"

She tried to reconcile his actions with the words coming out of his mouth. He put his life on hold to repair her business, moved to an apartment over the stables to make room for her family, and recalled her favorite ice cream. But he didn't love her—was only marking time until he could return to his life up in Ohio.

"I do. Just thinking."

She took a small bite, savoring the sweetness as it slid down her throat.

Luke touched the rim of her bowl. "I want to see all that gone. You didn't eat more than two bites back at the house."

"I shouldn't be eating dessert if I didn't finish my dinner." She let her spoon drop, irritated he was scolding her like a child.

He arched an eyebrow and put another spoonful in his mouth.

She wanted to lean across the table and kiss him, smug rascal that he was. Instead, she folded her arms, prepared to wait him out. If she wanted a lecture, there were two women at home…

He spooned another mouthful of chocolate to his lips, setting her stomach to rumbling. He had a point. She'd been living off antacids and protein bars. With so much in her life out of her control, what and how much she ate was one thing she could determine.

Time to see her therapist. She'd battled anorexia all through high school and hadn't gotten a handle on her eating until college when the stress of living with her parents had lessened. She'd realized then the disease was controlling her and not the other way around. She wouldn't let those old issues worm their way into her life again.

"You're right. I can't afford to get sick now." Or add more problems to her already full plate. She brought a spoonful to her lips, savoring the sweetness. Then the pain hit. She pressed a hand to her middle. If only her stomach would agree. *Damn ulcer.*

"You okay?"

Julia peered up at him. Rachel's words echoed in her mind. "Do you watch everything I do?"

"I try not to, but it's hard not to see you wasting away."

She tugged the windbreaker closed. "It's not something I take pleasure in." Although her mother made a point of telling her how great she looked in the dress she'd worn earlier. In her social circle, women still clung to long-held beliefs. A lady could never marry too rich—even if she didn't love the man—could never wear too much jewelry or could never be too thin. In fact, the anorexia years were the only time her mother ever complimented her appearance. "The thoughts of eating makes my stomach hurt." She took another spoonful, just to prove the desire to push away the bowl couldn't best her. "Except this. This is heaven."

"I remembered you liking this before."

"You remember a great deal for someone who doesn't care about me."

"I didn't say I don't *care* for you. I said I wasn't *good* for you. There's a difference."

They needed to lay down some ground rules if they were going to be in such proximity to each other. No more allowing him to fix things for her. Nor would she beg to be let in if he wouldn't share himself with her. She already loved him too much. Had given too much of her heart only to have him desert her again. "Luke, why did you bring me out here? It's obvious you don't want to be with me."

"I was trying to get you away from those two. Do you always let them bully you?"

"I'm usually better at managing the moms."

"It's good to know you can stand up to them."

Her temper simmered. She handled them and many other things quite well. She wasn't at her best today after the debacle the night before. "I need to tell you something."

"Please don't."

She held up a hand and shook her head. "It's not that. Believe me, I won't be making that mistake again." Her wounded pride couldn't take any more beatings.

He reached across the table, coming within an inch of her hand before pulling back. "I'm not the right guy for you, princess. You deserve so much more." His voice sounded ancient, far older, and harder than his thirty-odd years.

"That wasn't what you used to think. We made plans—good plans."

He looked away. "Things happen."

"What happened to change you?"

"Nothing good."

"Won't you tell me? I can see the hurt in your eyes."

He slowly rose from the bench. “I need to get you back. Your moms will be wondering where their ice cream is.”

She’d have found his phrasing humorous if it weren’t for the weight on her chest. “I just need to say one thing.” She met and held his gaze, something she found hard to do but very necessary in this moment. “Stop rescuing me.”

His jaw tightened. “I’ll bear that in mind the next time a tornado comes along.”

“That’s not what I meant, and you know it. I need you to stop fixing things. You’re not the only one who’s changed. I’m not that fragile girl you once knew.”

“Princess, you were never fragile. You’ve always had a backbone of steel. It was one of the things I liked best about you.”

Then he’d been able to see things she didn’t realize were there.

Looking back, she saw a vapid girl whose interests were looking nice and going to parties. Her horses were the only thing of substance in her world. Until Luke came into it.

He’d made her care about causes that had never been part of her reality. His disappearance crushed her, and she fell into old patterns to cope. Shopping, vacations, and the social circuit of Atlanta filled her world. Her marriage to Paul had been a disaster culminating in her father’s death and her affair. The discovery of Aiden’s hearing impairment awakened the dormant strength she needed to advocate for her son. It set her on the path to the woman she now was.

“That’s very kind of you to say.” Too bad it wasn’t

enough for him to give their love another try. "But as you say, much happened in our lives, and it's time I get back to mine."

As Julia clung to Luke on the ride back, she replayed their conversation. However, she returned to one part, dissecting each word. What had happened to change Luke and where did he go when he left Magnolia Valley?

Chapter Nine

The next day, the crunch of tires against gravel drew the attention of everyone in the stable, Luke's included. He propped the pitchfork against the wall and walked to the entrance in time to see a man exit the same luxury car that had delivered Mrs. Chandler and Mrs. Wilkes the day before. He tried to recall Paul Wilkes' face from years before and came up blank. Luke did remember the guy was a few grades ahead at Magnolia Valley High and had been a popular athlete.

Julia bolted out the front door. She made a beeline to the rear of the car where she quickly extricated a young boy. He pulled away from the opening. The happy family scene was one he didn't need to witness. Even as he attended to the mundane tasks around the farm, his thoughts remained on the reunion beyond the stable walls. Voices drifted in. He turned up the music on his phone to drown out the sweet sound of Julia's laughter.

Over the years he'd fixated on how different his life could have been. His parents would have kept the farm. He would have gone on to practice veterinary medicine. Maybe he and Julia would have married. However, if he hadn't answered his sister's plea for help, she certainly would have died that night. When he'd been desperate to regain what had been lost, he reminded himself the five years in prison were a small price to pay for Yvonne's life. That knowledge didn't stop him from wallowing in regret from time to time. Accomplishing his goal of buying back the family farm should have offered more satisfaction. In fact, the deep longing that drove him forward all these years seemed to intensify.

His thoughts rewound to the clusterfuck of two nights ago. He owed Julia a better explanation than the piss poor one he'd offered. Perhaps if he squared things with her, made her understand unlike the family farm, their love could not be reclaimed, he could leave Magnolia Valley in peace.

How would he do that without revealing he was a murderer?

Luke could take Julia believing him a jerk for disappearing years ago or think him callous for pushing her away now. The possibility she might look at him with fear cut him to the core. It shouldn't since it was many people's reaction. Hell, most of the time it was what he wanted to see in others. He loved she saw past the tattoos, piercings, and his size to the man he'd once been—however little of him there was left. To keep that look in her eyes, he'd do whatever it took to keep his secret buried.

****

Julia knelt, her eyes roaming over Aiden. Her six-year-old appeared to have grown an inch in the week since she'd seen him.

Mommy is so happy you're here.

Aiden's hands formed the sign for barn then horse.

Her heart ached. How much did the little boy understand about Pumpkin's death?

In a little while. Let's go inside and see your new

room.

Julia steered Aiden in the direction of the house. *Your grandmothers are inside waiting to see you. They're going to live here with us. They've planned a picnic this afternoon.*

Aiden refused to move, emphatically repeating the two signs.

Julia let out a breath and smiled. "Should have known you wouldn't be distracted." After returning her son's bags to the car trunk, she took him by the hand. *I guess the grandmothers will just have to wait.*

Paul joined them, hefting Aiden into his arms. "Speaking of the grand dames, thanks again for letting mine come up here. Did she do all right last night? Not too grumpy I hope."

"She was fine. I'm glad she could keep my mother company."

Putting up with her third degree, not so much.

The conversation with them following her bike ride with Luke had been a real joy. "I'm afraid there's not going to be much for the two of them to do up here besides doting on Aiden." And grilling her about Luke. Many of the queries Julia would have been all too happy to know the answer herself.

"Don't be surprised if she's more of a challenge than usual. Moving out of her home has unsettled her."

"Why is that? She knows it's temporary."

"Mom takes great comfort in living in the expensive house I bought her. That way she can pretend our early days didn't exist."

While Julia's family depended on ancestral wealth. Paul worked for the money he so generously shared with his family. What began as a crop-dusting operation in a broken-down hangar was now one of Atlanta's many entrepreneur success stories.

"Then she really is a good friend to my mother to come up here. I'll try to bear that in mind when the two gang up on me." *Again.*

As they reached the barn, Aiden wiggled free from his dad's arms and raced to the nearest stall. He scrambled up a hay bale to peer inside, noted the resident then moved to the next spot.

"You think he's looking for Pumpkin?" Paul asked.

"Probably." How much did six-year-olds understand of death?

Paul shifted his weight from foot to foot. "Michelle and I did like we discussed. Every time Aiden asked about the pony, we sign the same thing, Pumpkin died and is in heaven with Pickles the Cat and his grandpas."

"I'm sure you did fine." Julia patted him on the shoulder. "He just needs to work this out for himself."

"Can't you distract him or something?" He pointed to their son as he continued his search. "He's killing me, here."

"I'll see what I can do." Julia walked over to Aiden, praying this tactic would work.

Would you like to see a surprise, sweetheart?

Aiden stilled long enough to sign *candy*.

This is even better. Misty had her baby. Would you like to see her foul?

The little boy's face lit up.

"I think we have success," Julia called to Paul. "Want to come see?"

He joined them, scooping Aiden into his arms as they stood outside the stall. "How does he walk on those spindly legs?"

"I know what you mean." Julia kept her voice low to not disturb the new mother and baby.

Aiden, what should we name him?

"Anything but Candy," Paul said. "I'll never know what or who he wants."

She chuckled, grateful for an easy conversation. Their relationship hadn't always been so. Thanks to counseling and a lot of maturing on her part, they'd found a way to be a family. A cordial relationship with her ex didn't preclude her from a small amount of envy now that Paul had found happiness with his new wife. And she was pining after Luke, wondering why he insisted on keeping his distance.

What do you say to changing into your boots then saddling up Penny?

Julia hoped to keep the boy from resuming his search for Pumpkin and her from dwelling on futile subjects.

Miss Lisa will be here in a little while to give you a lesson.

Aiden took off at full tilt, scurrying to the Shetland's stall. He unlatched the door and had the pony by the halter before his parents could catch up.

"What is he doing?" Paul's voice raised an octave. "Stop him. He's going to get hurt."

"He's fine." Julia stifled a laugh. If Paul had his way, their son would be dressed in bubble-wrap armor and would wear his helmet twenty-four/seven instead of just during riding lessons. He worried Aiden's hearing impairment made riding more dangerous. Then again, he thought that about T-ball, swimming, and gymnastics.

Let's get Penny's saddle and bridle.

Julia helped Aiden tack the horse and led the animal to the small ring at the far end of the barn. When the boy trotted off on his mount, she turned to Paul. "He'll be fine. I swear. Penny's every bit as gentle as Pumpkin was." The whine of a truck engine broke into her reassurance speech. "I bet that's Miss Lisa now. Stay and watch. You'll see what an excellent equestrian our son is becoming."

"Thanks. I'd like that."

The two of them leaned against the wooden fencing as Aiden's instructor joined her student in the ring. "How's business?" Julia asked. "Did the insurance company finally pay out for the airplane you lost?"

"They did." Paul's attention never left his son as Aiden trotted from one end of the ring to the other. "Profits are back on track, no thanks to that damned tornado. You?"

"Things are coming along. The contractor I hired is working miracles on the place." And keeping her up at night with questions.

The hairs on the back of Julia's neck stood as Luke approached from behind. Her heart rate sped up. Cheeks heated. God, the last thing she needed was for Paul to clue into her feelings for Luke. She willed her body to calm. Could she even risk looking at him? She thumbed over her shoulder. "Paul, do you remember Luke Chevalier?" She kept her voice as smooth as her favorite silk blouse. "I believe you two were at Magnolia Valley High at the same time."

Her ex's gaze widened, cut back to Aiden, and then refocused on Luke as if he couldn't decide which threat to track. "The name sounds familiar."

"I've changed a bit over the years." Luke offered

his hand to Paul, bringing him into her sightline.

Julia bit back a gasp. He'd *changed.*

Back were the ear gauges and brow piercings, and the tattoos were in full view beneath the tank top. The skull trim made a reappearance, replacing the inch-long growth he'd allowed. All reminders to her no doubt.

"He moved back to Magnolia Valley the day of the tornado."

"My stay here is temporary." He pointed to the barn behind them. "I've wanted to repurchase my family's farm ever since it was sold twelve years ago. I only came to sign the paperwork."

"He's stayed on to oversee the repairs to Highlands."

Paul crossed his arms. "So, you'll leave again as soon as it's complete?"

"Absolutely, I have work waiting on me in Ohio."

Paul's phone rang. "That's Michelle. I need to get this." He stepped away but continued to cast his gaze toward Julia and Luke every few seconds.

"Did you need something from me?" Julia asked.

He shrugged. "Just checking on Misty and the foal."

"Uh-huh. I know what you're doing."

"You do, do you?"

She stabbed a finger in his direction. "If the tats and piercings didn't scare me off when you first returned home, they're not going to now."

"First." He held up a finger. "This isn't my home." Then he held his arms out wide. "Second, this is the real me. Last night was a show of respect for the dinner invitation extended by Mrs. Chandler and Mrs. Wilkes."

Julia closed the distance, frustration boiling inside her. "I can see the good person you still are on the inside." His grimace softened, giving her hope. "Won't you let me in?"

Luke stiffened his arm, preventing her from embracing him.

"What?" she asked in confusion.

"Your ex would really like to come over here. I believe he's contemplating ripping my arms off."

"No, he's not." She turned to study Paul who was indeed scowling in their direction. "This is none of his business," she said loud enough for her voice to carry. "He's got enough of his own worries to focus on."

Luke's dark chuckle warmed her insides. "Is there any man who isn't jockeying for position to be your cavalier? I do believe you're the twenty-first century version of Scarlet O'Hara."

Julia let out a huff. "If there is a line, they're all wasting their time, and if memory serves me correctly, Scarlet took care of business herself."

He raised his hands in surrender. "I'm just teasing, princess. No need to get upset."

"I told you before, I'm looking for someone to share my life with, not a man to make all my problems go away." Angry tears welled in her eyes, and she turned so he couldn't see her brush them away.

"Everything alright?" Paul asked.

She forced a smile to her lips. "Sure, why wouldn't they be?"

Worry lined his eyes. "That was Michelle on the phone. She's back home from the baby shower she was attending, so I'm going to say goodbye to Aiden and my mom."

As Paul headed toward the ring, Luke said, "You're still quite close to your ex's family."

"They're Aiden's family. They'll always be a part of my life."

"But you don't want to be with Paul?" He reached for a nearby pitchfork and leaned against the handle.

"No." She managed to destroy their marriage with her infidelity. "He's remarried a wonderful woman who loves my son dearly."

"So, what happened?"

Julia arched an eyebrow. "You're not the only one with topics best left in the past."

Luke nodded. "Point taken." He stabbed the pitchfork into the hay bale. "Anyway, I've got chores to do in the barn. Holler if you need anything."

"Can those wait?" Her chest tightened with anxiety.

"Sure. What do you need?"

"I want to introduce you to Aiden."

"Umm." He tugged on his shirttail and ran a palm over his scalp.

"Only if you want to. I just thought…" God, why did she think this was a good idea? It wasn't like Aiden would be in the barn by himself.

"No, no. Like I said before, I'd love to meet your son."

"Come find us in a while. Aiden's lesson will be ending shortly."

He backed away. "I'll check on Misty in the meantime."

Soon after Paul left for Atlanta, Julia followed her son as he led his pony from the riding ring to the barn.

Did you have a good time on Penny?

Aiden grinned. *More.*

Julia laughed. *Later on today we'll go for a ride. First, you need some lunch, and then I want you to see your new bedroom.*

"Is now a good time?" Luke closed the tack room door behind him. He'd changed into jeans and a long-sleeved shirt, pulling a ball cap down low on his head.

Her heart warmed at the accommodations he'd made. "Absolutely. He takes a while to warm up to new people, so don't be offended if he doesn't make eye contact or hides behind my legs.

Luke dropped to his knees. "That's okay. I'm not sure about new people, either."

Julia's breath caught as Luke began signing. *Hi, Aiden, my name is Luke.* His fingers were slow as he spelled out his name. *I'm a friend of your mom's.*

Aiden gave a shy wave then hid on the other side of his pony.

"I didn't know you knew sign language."

"I don't." He glanced up. "I started learning when you told me Aiden was hearing impaired."

Her throat tightened. "You did that for us?"

"I thought it would be a good idea in case he needed to tell me something." He looked away. "I hope that's okay."

She nodded, unable to speak. How was she supposed to keep her distance from a man who repeatedly went to great lengths to make her life better? "That's more than okay. It's everything."

Chapter Ten

Following a quiet weekend settling into Luke's farmhouse, Julia's Monday morning to-do list filled two pages. After a delay, her formal pitch to Richard stood at number one, but would take place after she settled several personnel issues.

In the newly refurbished hotel kitchen, she stood before her head chef. "Hector, I don't know what I'm going to do without you. You're sure I can't convince you to hang on a little longer? We'll be up and running soon." Guilt tore at her. How could she expect people to go without pay? She'd dipped into her meager savings to keep a few key employees on the payroll, but that money had run out last week. Between her mother's upkeep and loan payments, she'd be lucky to survive until the grand reopening.

He tugged on his shirt collar. "You've been so good to me, Ms. Wilkes. I'll never forget everything you've done for me, but my family needs…"

Julia waved away his explanation. "Say no more. I completely understand you have greater obligations than to me." She extended her hand. "I wish you the very best luck in your new position."

Hector blushed through his dark complexion. "My family and I will keep you in our prayers."

She needed every prayer she could get. A completed building was worthless without a high-caliber staff to run it. "Thank you. I'll see you out."

As they walked through the corridor leading to the main lobby, she studied the workmanship—not that she didn't trust Luke to do a good job. She needed the reassurance progress was being made. New electricity had been installed, the front desk remodeled, and the new, upscale décor turned out exactly how she envisioned. Highlands would be better than ever, especially if she could convince Richard to finally open his checkbook at their scheduled meeting.

Reaching the parking lot, Julia fixed a smile to her face. "If the new place isn't to your liking, you always have employment here."

Before she could return to her office, or get her pity party started, Rachel pulled into the parking lot. Her second-in-command called over the weekend asking for a meeting. Though she suspected the reason for the drive up from Atlanta, Julia couldn't contain her joy at seeing her dear friend. She danced over to Rachel's SUV, embracing the woman as she exited. "You're a sight for sore eyes."

"You, too." Rachel pushed a strand of her long, brown hair behind her ear. "How's it going?"

Julia took in her friend's broad smile. "You're glowing. Are you pregnant?"

"No." Rachel rolled her eyes.

"Then it's Brad. He's heard about the teaching job."

"We can talk about that later."

Her heart sank. *Another loss.* Yet, she couldn't resent her friend for wanting her husband to have a job that kept him out of harm's way. "Okay, after the presentation, we'll have lunch and catch up."

They slowed their walk as they reached the front of the freshly finished façade. Rachel ran her hand over one of the *porte-cochére 's* columns. "It's looking even better than before. How much longer until it's finished?"

"Luke says it'll be six weeks."

"Speaking of tall, dark, and scary, how's it going with him?"

Awful, gut-wrenching, wonderful—depending on the moment.

"Like you said, we can talk about that later."

Aiden had taken to him, something that had never happened before. Luke continued to amaze her with his progress in learning ASL. He'd joined them for dinner again last night where he charmed her mother. Yet, he rebuffed all Julia's attempts to spend time alone with her.

They settled into Julia's office like old times, with Rachel dragging a chair around the desk so the women sat side-by-side. The presentation needed a few minor adjustments then they moved on to future bookings. "I've confirmed with all our events for July. The Wilson/Maccabee wedding will be our first, with the golf tournament the next weekend."

Rachel leaned back in her chair. "It'll be like the tornado never happened. You'll be right where you were before."

Julia let out a breath. "Fingers crossed, Richard can take me to the next level."

"What time is he getting here again?"

"Three. It's supposed to rain later this afternoon, so I'm going to give him the golf cart tour of the grounds first." Déjà vu creeped up her spine. That had been her plan the day the tornado ripped through her world. "After that, we'll go over my numbers, the asking price for Wolfe Winery, and my projections for the expansion costs."

"Good idea." Rachel steepled her fingers. "Can I give my opinion on something?"

"Of course."

"First, that man is a little too slick for my liking. Second, he wants to be more than your business partner."

"Wow, tell me what you really think." Joking aside, Julia weighed her friend's comments. She'd known Richard socially for years, and among their group he had a stellar reputation for good business decisions. She also trusted Rachel's bullshit meter. On the other hand, Rachel was no fan of Luke's, who Julia trusted with the most precious thing in her life—Aiden.

The woman shrugged. "You know me; I tell it like it is."

"It's one of the many things I love about you, and I'll bear in mind what you said about Richard's character."

None of the women in her Atlanta social circle understood her drive the way Rachel did. Sure, they were interested in money, but their way of accumulating wealth was to marry it, not earn it for themselves.

"And about Richard wanting to date you, have you cued into that?"

"He's dropped more than a few clues, and I've tried to make myself feel something romantic for him. I just don't."

"How about Luke, do you have a thing for him?"

"He's only here long enough to finish this job, and then he's going back to Ohio," Julia stated, as much to herself as to Rachel.

"That's not an answer. What's going on between you and Luke?"

Julia leaned back. "Who said anything's going on between us?"

"No one had to say anything. It's the way he looks at you. Plus, you blossom every time he's near."

"Okay, I admit, I have feelings for Luke, but it's all one sided."

"I don't know about that." Rachel cocked her head. "I don't think he would have changed his plans if he didn't have some feelings for you."

"He has a hero complex, that's all. I've told him I don't want him around so he can fix my problems. Anyway, that's enough about me." She met Rachel's gaze. "When does Brad start his new job?"

A small smile played at Rachel's lips. "Not for several weeks. He's turned in his notice, so he'll be free by the end of the month for us to go down there to house hunt. He starts teaching in August."

That gave her enough time to plan a farewell party. "We'll just have to make the most of the time we do have."

"You're not upset?"

"Upset?" Her voice rose. "I'm heart broken. Who else is going to tell me when my skirt is tucked into my pantyhose or I've got spinach in my teeth? But the big girl panties are firmly in place."

She chuckled. "Do you need me to hang around while the investor is here?"

"No. I know you want to get started packing up the

cottage. Wish me luck, though."

Rachel waggled her finger. "Keep in mind what I said about Richard."

"I will, and I'll let you know how our meeting goes." They walked together through the hotel corridors until they parted ways at the rear entrance. As always, she scanned the area for Luke. Catching sight of him by a large materials truck, she headed his way. He and his crew hefted sheets of drywall off the truck, stacking them against the side of the hotel. "It's supposed to rain later."

He nodded as he passed a load to the waiting arms of a worker. "Which is why we're moving this inside as soon as I've made sure the supplier isn't shorting you again."

"Oh." How had that escaped her notice? She reviewed every invoice he showed her. Thank God for Luke, again. Although as contractor, supervising was in his job description. Where would the rebuild be if he hadn't taken her on? Certainly not in a position for her to pitch to Richard.

Luke tugged her out of earshot of his crew. "You look worried. Is it investor guy? Did he cancel?"

"No, he'll be here in a little while." She smoothed the worry lines that must be evident on her face.

"Don't worry about the third floor. I know it doesn't look like it, but Highlands will be ready for its grand reopening."

Julia rubbed at the knot in her sternum. "Not if I keep losing employees it won't. My chef quit this morning, and Rachel just turned in her notice. Her husband took a job teaching at a college in South Georgia."

"You can always hire more people."

"Can't hire friends though. Rachel's the one person I can count on to give it to me straight. Plus, she's a good sounding board."

"You can talk to me if you like." His amber eyes rooted her, drew her, comforted her.

She shook herself loose from their tender bonds. In a few weeks, he'd be out of her life again. "Thanks, but you've got enough on your shoulders already." She'd made a vow not to let him rescue her anymore.

"I think I can handle it. Tell me about this expansion plan you need the investor for. What's wrong with the way things are now? Highlands looks terrific the way it is. Or at least before the tornado got to it."

"I thought so myself for a while after the initial remodel. Revenue was good, and I was booked solid for the rest of the year. I could easily coast for a while, but it's not the vision I have for my resort. When I was a teenager my parents took me to France. It was glorious. The vineyards were something to behold. I never wanted to leave. That's what I want for Highlands. People could drive up from Atlanta to spend a weekend and feel like they've been to Europe or Napa."

"I'm impressed."

"You're the *only* one."

"Seems like your family should be in your corner."

"Paul's supportive of the resort, but says I should concentrate on my core business, weddings. And you've heard what the moms think."

"Don't listen to them. They've got their own interests in mind. Tell Pierce what you told me. He'll see your passion and be writing a check before the day is over, and if he doesn't, just find someone who sees your vision."

She soaked up his praise. "God, I needed to hear that." On impulse she hugged him. "You always know the right thing to say."

He stiffened but didn't pull out of the embrace. "I'm only telling you how I see it, princess."

Richard's arrival prevented anything further. His luxury import edged around to the rear parking lot. "Wish me luck."

"*Bonne chance.*"

Julia met the investor by the side of his car. "What do you think of the progress we've made?" She gestured toward the front of the hotel to draw his attention away from the ongoing construction.

He pushed his sunglasses to the top of his head. "The outside looks better than new. Exterior, landscaping, if I hadn't been here, I'd never have guessed the devastation."

The butterflies in her stomach settled. "I'm glad you think so. The first and second floors are done as well."

He hooked her arm with his. "Shall we see it together first?"

"Not yet." She resisted his pull. "You need to see the exterior changes to grasp my vision for the winery. Besides, I believe I owe you a tour of my golf course."

A cool smile creased his face. "By all means. Lead on, my dear lady."

Julia slid into the driver's seat and as soon as Richard had settled, took off down the path toward the back of her property. "My plans for the golf course have been altered slightly due to the loss of so many trees. The designer has taken that into consideration and made the necessary changes."

"I'm sure it'll be everything you say."

"Your capital will propel Highlands into world class status." That might be a bit of an exaggeration but if she didn't sell her idea who would? She drove along the path, pointing out the areas where the new design would alter the course and the repairs to the cottages Luke had completed. At the back of the property she stopped the cart. The butterflies started up another swarm. "Topher's been in contact, offered a fair price. He and Cristobel plan to retire to Florida."

"How are your bookings for the summer?"

"They're good. We've got weddings every weekend through October. I'm taking out an ad in *Destination* magazine. I'd like to be able to add the winery to our list of amenities."

He nodded. "Staff? Where are you with filling vacant positions?"

"I've lost some loyal employees, I admit. I'm certain with an influx of capital, I'll be able to recruit topnotch people again."

"I think I've seen enough. Let's head back to your office."

They made the return trip in silence. The second guessing and tense anticipation sucked the breath out of her. By the time they reached the back of the hotel, her head was pounding.

"Stop."

Julia jolted after such a long stretch of quiet. "What?"

He gestured to Luke as he sent his crew scurrying in different directions. "That man you were talking to, he's your contractor, right?"

She swallowed hard. Had he seen them embrace? "Yes, Luke Chevalier."

"Tell me again where you found this guy. He looks more like a gang member than a contractor."

The urge to jump to Luke's defense clawed at her. "He's bonded, licensed, and his references are excellent. Not only that, he's on time and under budget."

His gaze cut to Luke. "So you say, but I think he bears watching."

His words cut to her heart, more a threat than an expression of concern for her wellbeing.

"I know you have other clients who need your attention, so let's focus on our business." She steered him toward the hotel's rear entrance. "Why don't we move to my office where we can look over my documents?"

He brought her hand to his lips. The touch to her flesh sent shivers across her skin, but not in a good way. "None of my other clients are as lovely as you. Nor do they hold my interest the way you do. A little more privacy sounds perfect."

Oh, Lord. Even the most naïve could predict what he had in mind. When he tugged on her arm, she dug in her heels. "Richard, we need to talk. I think—"

"You think too much."

Lovely smile, gentle voice, spine of steel.

Screw the first two parts.

"Listen. You've gotten the wrong idea about us. I value your help immeasurably, but I think it would be best if we kept our relationship *strictly professional.*" Surely, in the twenty-first century women weren't still choosing between accepting unwanted male attention and caring for their family?

His nostrils flared. "I see. Is it the contractor? Are you involved with him?"

Julia folded her arms. "I'm not involved with anyone and don't expect to be for the foreseeable future. Work and my son are my focus." She could see the wheels inside his head turning.

The cool smile made a return appearance. "Strictly professional, it is."

She let out a breath but found she couldn't quite relax. Men like him didn't admit defeat easily. "I can email you the latest financial documents along with the final numbers for the winery purchase if you'd prefer."

Richard tugged at his shirt cuffs. "Perhaps that would be best. I suddenly recall another appointment."

Julia followed him to his car, willing calm and refusing to explain. "When can I expect your decision about your investment?"

After shutting the door, he lowered the window and leaned through the opening. "You've given me a lot to think about. I'll give you my decision as soon as I've made it. His car trundled down the drive, leaving defeat in his wake.

She chewed at a hangnail. In the distance, she caught sight of Luke's white T-shirt. He'd offered to lend an ear… "No, this is my little red wagon to pull. I'm not going to him for help, and I'm sure not selling myself—come hell or high water."

But had the rebuff cost her everything she'd worked so hard for?

Chapter Eleven

Several days later, the afternoon sun beat down on Luke's shoulders. After years confined to concrete and metal, he never missed an opportunity to view the sky. Heat be damned. He wadded up the waxed paper he'd used to wrap his sandwich and tossed it back in the cooler. "Back to it."

He stretched as he stood then replaced the iron patio chair underneath its tarp before heading back inside. Except for the new barn going up on the other side of the knoll, the exterior was complete. So was a good chunk of the interior. As he mentally ticked off the remaining tasks, the hairs on the back of his neck stood at attention. On instinct, his fists clenched, and his arms drew into a defensive position. He turned. "Mr. Pierce, Ms. Wilkes isn't here."

"I'm aware of that. It's you I came to see."

Something about the man's smirk made him think he wouldn't be asking about drywall or light fixtures. "What can I do for you?"

"I have a few questions, if you don't mind."

Luke kept his face neutral and his words civil for Julia's sake, when what he really wanted to do was tell the guy to go fuck himself. "Shoot."

"Mrs. Chandler tells me she and Julia are living in the house on your property."

Ahh, so that's what this is about.

Hot Shot wanted to mark his territory. Luke folded his arms across his chest. Let the little dog bark. "That's a statement not a question."

Pierce's jaw ticked. "How do you like living in a barn?"

"I've had worse neighbors than D'Artagnan."

He snatched off his sunglasses, a scowl marring the fucker's too handsome face. "That horse is a monster that ought to be put down."

Perhaps the enemy of my enemy is *my friend.* "He's not so bad once you get to know him."

"It's awfully generous of you to uproot yourself so soon after buying back your family's farm." Pierce removed his straw fedora, using it to fan himself.

So, he'd been the topic of conversation. What else did Pierce know? Tension coiled inside him. It wouldn't do for the fucker to start digging. He seemed the sort to object to hiring ex-cons. "Again, not a question. Do you have one for me, or are you fact checking the article you're writing for *Gun and Bloom*?"

His face turned florid. Beads of perspiration trickled down his cheeks and underneath the buttoned collar of his shirt. "I can see you're every bit the ruffian Mrs. Chandler says you are."

Did Julia know her future business partner had been talking to her mother? "And here I thought the lady and I were getting on so well. She certainly found my wine selection appealing."

"I'll come right to the point." Pierce jerked his sleeves in place. "What is the nature of your relationship with *my* Julia?"

Mine!

No, she wasn't his any more than she belonged to the Rhett Butler wannabe who stood before him. "We're contractor and client, or landlord and tenant if you prefer." He couldn't even claim friendship, despite what the raging beast inside him insisted. Not for lack of him wanting things to be different.

During the first year of his sentence, he'd spent the long, lonely nights replaying every conversation they'd ever had. He relived each ride they'd taken together and time they'd made love. Now he had to settle for watching her from his apartment window. Her smiles, those had to be enough. The thoughts of returning to those cold, sunless days filled him with dread, but once the project was complete his reasons for staying in Magnolia Valley would run out.

"Good to know." Richard stroked his chin. "So, from veterinarian student to construction. That's quite a stretch."

"What can I say? I'm a man of many talents." He leaned in a bit, taking pleasure in watching the bastard take a step back. "I assure you my credentials are in order. I'd be happy to show you the paperwork if you like."

"That won't be necessary." Pierce tugged on his collar. "God, the heat out here is oppressive. Let's continue this conversation inside."

When he headed toward the hotel's back entrance, Luke caught him by the jacket. "No can do. Too much scaffolding and shit still up in there. Wouldn't do to have you getting hurt."

Pierce jerked loose from Luke's grasp. "Julia says she's been working out of her office for the past week. You're not putting her in a situation where she could get injured, are you?"

Luke reined in his temper. "The lady knows how to take care of herself." He'd also made her promise to stay in her office and use a back entrance where the construction was complete, but Dicky-boy didn't need to know that.

"How much longer until the remodeling is finished?"

Finally, a question he didn't mind answering. He had the days marked on the calendar. He both longed for and dreaded when he no longer had a legitimate excuse for seeing her. "Barring any unforeseen incidents, my crew should be done with the main building in three weeks. The stables should be complete soon after."

"That's good news." A smile creased his face. "Julia is working entirely too much. I think when all this craziness is over, I'll take her on a little getaway."

"Getaway?" Luke barked a laugh. What world was his guy living in? "Don't you think she'll be a little too busy with the reopening?"

"That's what she has staff for. Some friends of ours have invited us to their house in Bermuda." Richard toyed with the stem of his sunglasses.

"Do you take all your clients on vacation?"

"We're much more than that. Not only do we have a great deal in common, but our families have moved in the same social circles for generations. Her Uncle Hemi went to school with my Grandfather Robinson."

Pierce might as well have presented Luke with his stud papers. Rich folks had come from all over the Atlanta area to board their horses at his parents' stables. His father sold them the best Selle Français stock

Rockaway Farm could produce, and his mom had taught their children how to ride.

"If you know Julia as well as you claim, you'd know how important Highlands is to her. She's not going to be willing to turn over the reins to an assistant to go on vacation with you."

"I don't think there's going to be a great deal here to keep her occupied."

"You're not going to come through for her?" Luke's gut twisted. Julia would be devastated if Pierce refused to invest in her new venture. Other than Aiden, all she talked about was her plans for Highlands's expansion.

Pierce shrugged. "I have a few loose ends to tie up, and my due diligence to complete before I make my final decision."

Luke wanted to punch the guy and screw the repercussions. "You're not in favor of her expansion plans?" He'd heard them and thought they were brilliant. "If she gets the backing, Highlands could be the next Chateau Elan. Don't you want her to be a success?"

Though she hadn't said as much, he got the impression Highlands wasn't merely a diverting hobby. Perhaps the Chandlers weren't as well off as they once were.

"I think her talents lie elsewhere. I can take care of her. Keep her and her family in the style they were born to."

Luke's eyes widened. He didn't realize dinosaurs still roamed Georgia. "What if she wants to take care of herself?"

"With any luck, she'll get passed this independent

phase and see sense."

Luke had heard enough. He had to get the hell out of there, otherwise he might be tempted to pound some feminism into the fucker. "If that's all the questions you've got for me, I've got some work to do."

Pierce flashed another smug smile. "Don't let me keep you."

He jutted out his hand. "Nice chatting. Good luck convincing Julia to take a vacation." He clamped down on the guy's palm before releasing it.

Luke stalked off toward the stables. He had work he could be doing inside, but right now he needed to get physical with something. Driving nails into wood would have to do since he couldn't pound the little shit into the ground.

"Here, let me have that." He took a hammer from one of his crew who was hanging siding for the new barn. Working alongside the guys allowed him to lose himself in the monotony of measure, cut, hammer, and repeat. Thank God, several rows later his temper was under control. "I'll help you get this last board hung, and then I've got to see how the boys are doing inside."

"Sure thing, boss," said the young kid who'd worked silently alongside him. "You're welcome to come down here anytime. I think you've done most of my work for me."

Luke let out a laugh as he laid down the hammer. "Should I dock your pay, then?" Again, he sensed another's presence behind him. This time, however, the breeze carried her perfume. A tingle of awareness shot up his spine. "You missed Richie Rich."

Julia stepped into his sightline. Dressed in a robin's egg colored suit, she appeared to have come directly from a meeting down in Atlanta. "Really? I wasn't expecting him. Did he say what he wanted?"

"Let's talk over here." He drew her over to the far end of the paddock out of earshot of the crew. "He had a few questions for me." Should he warn her Pierce had a version of support that didn't match hers? Would she resent Luke interfering in her professional life? Like they needed another wedge between them.

He already kept two truths from her. First, the reason for his disappearance a dozen years ago. Second, his love for her had never dimmed. In everything else he had to be scrupulously honest. "He mentioned something about taking you on a vacation."

She pressed a palm to her temple. "He does not listen to a word I say. I told him I wanted to keep things strictly professional. I guess I didn't get through to him."

Luke wanted to cheer. "I can help you with that if you like."

"I've got it." She waved away his offer. "He just has to get used to the idea."

"Do you think he's still going to come through with the money?" What would she do if Pierce backed out? God, he'd give anything to be the one to help her realize her vision for Highlands.

"He hasn't made up his mind. I'm trying to stay positive, but I honestly can't say for sure which way he's leaning."

"When will he let you know?"

Julia chewed her lip. "Soon, I hope. He wanted to crunch the numbers one more time." She let out a breath. "Anyway, I had a great meeting in Atlanta with the people from *Brides' World*. I'll be participating in their expo next February, so I feel like celebrating. What say we have some lunch?"

"You're eating? This I've got to see."

She rolled her eyes at him. "I've been careful about my caloric intake, at least twelve hundred a day. Thank you very much."

He wanted to wipe her impish grin off her face, with his lips. "Good to hear."

"I've got an idea." She tapped her finger to her lips. "Let's go for a ride. D'Artagnan needs a workout. We can take a picnic lunch like we used to."

"I can't. Not if you want this place open in three weeks." Certainly not if he had planned to keep his hands off her.

"You're right." She hung her head, cutting him to the core. "I don't want to keep you from your work. I'm sorry I asked. I have plenty to do myself with the roommates coming back from their shopping trip later today."

Julia got inside her car and drove off, leaving him wondering why getting what he wanted caused such a sharp pain in his chest?

Chapter Twelve

Once inside Marie Chevalier's kitchen with its rooster wallpaper, Julia put steaks into marinate and tossed a salad for dinner. Halfway through assembling a berry tart, the doorbell rang. She dusted off her flour-covered hands on her jeans and walked into the living room. "Who could that be?" Paul wouldn't be bringing Aiden until later that night and the moms had a key.

Luke stood on the other side, his brows drawn tight together. He'd swapped his usual ball cap and T-shirt for a Stetson and chambray shirt.

"What's wrong? Did someone get hurt?"

"No." He raised a bag from a local sandwich shop. "Get your boots on."

"You don't have to." She wasn't some spoiled child who needed appeasing. "I know you've got a lot on your plate."

"That horse of yours needs exercising. I don't want to hear him stomping around in his stall all night."

She smiled, seeing through the bluster. Despite his barriers and secrets, remnants of his love for her still lingered. "We can't have that." She stood aside and motioned him in. "I won't be but a moment."

"I'll wait out here."

She blew out a breath. How many times had he joined her and the moms for dinner? "Oh, for crying out loud, come in out of the heat."

He took a couple steps over the threshold then stopped. *Did he think she would throw herself at him?* "Let me take care of a couple things in the kitchen, and I'll be ready." Jeez, she had some pride. Hadn't her confession in his apartment been enough of a battery to her ego?

After stowing the pastry dough in the refrigerator and grabbing her four-legged babies their treats, she returned to the living room. "All set."

"Boots?" Luke pointed to her sneakers.

"In the tack room. Mother despises their lingering odor." When she lived at Oakton, her mother had required Julia keep her riding habits in a locked trunk in the garage.

As she followed him onto the porch, happier memories of those days flooded back. Her gaze scanned the pasture ahead. Back then, they'd been adept at finding hidden knolls and shady spots to make love, not that she expected that would happen today. His volunteering to spend time with her was practically a miracle.

Heat radiated off him as they walked side-by-side to the barn. "D'Artagnan will appreciate getting to stretch his legs." Conversation was her attempt to keep her thoughts away from what it would be like to again find herself enveloped his enormous arms.

"I'm not holding my breath for any expressions of gratitude."

A laugh bubbled up inside her. "Probably a good idea."

Grazing several yards apart from the others, D'Artagnan lifted his head. Julia whistled as she crawled between the strands of deactivated electric fence. Cupping her hands to her mouth, she called, "Treats."

D'Artagnan thundered toward her with the mares trotting behind. She stood in the open, shaking her head, as her boy bore down on her. The kink in his long, flowing tail testified to his spirited mood and the ride she'd have. He came to a halt a foot in front of her and snorted. "Oh, all right. A promise is a promise."

Luke shook his head. "He acts like he wants to eat everyone else in the world, but you have Satan's minion eating out of your hand."

D'Artagnan nudged her, asking for his sugar cube.

"Literally."

She chuckled as she fished the treat out of her pocket. "You know your mama loves you, don't you?"

With the sugar gone, D'Artagnan rolled his eyes in Luke's direction and backed his ears.

Luke raised his hands. "It wasn't my idea to take you from your leisure. Take that up with her."

Julia took D'Artagnan by the halter and led him toward the barn. "Monster will come when you call her." She pointed to a large Palomino. "You should ride her." They'd make a good pair, a six-foot, four-inch man on a horse who stood seventeen hands.

He turned mumbling something that sounded like, "Name for the wrong horse."

After tacking the stallion, she led him to the entrance facing the open pasture. "I'll wait for you outside."

Luke nodded as he adjusted Monster's blanket then added a western saddle. "Be right there."

About the time D'Artagnan was getting antsy, Luke emerged from the barn. Grabbing the saddle's horn, he swung onto Monster's back in one fluid motion, like he'd never left Rockaway Farm. A sense of rightness filled her heart. "It's been a minute since we've done this."

His scowl returned. "Let's take them around the blackberry bushes and down to the creek." He nudged the horse on. "You can eat your sandwich there."

Her stomach knotted. Maybe the recollections were best kept to herself. She urged her horse forward. "Nice weather we're having. Perfect for growing hay."

"Sorry." He waited for her to catch up. "I don't mean to bite your head off or put you off when you want to talk about the past. It's not easy for me to remember how things were back then."

Why, if they were the best years of your life?

With the open pasture ahead, D'Artagnan took the bit in his teeth, anxious for a run. She reined him in as other questions tumbled toward her lips. "You must miss your parents terribly."

He nodded. "I wish they'd lived to see me buy back the farm."

Her heart ached for him. With their horses side-by-side, she bridged the gap between them, touching his arm. "Won't you please tell me what happened back then? I can't imagine—"

"There's no use talking about the past." He cut the air with his hand. "What's done is done. Hashing it over won't change a thing." He spurred the horse and took off at a gallop.

Luke was wrong. She'd taken great pains to examine the root cause of her failed marriage, so she wouldn't make the same mistakes if she ever found someone she wanted to share her life with. However, if a husband was all she wanted, Richard would have a ring on her finger before she could say, "pre-nuptial agreement."

Luke's blue shirt grew smaller as he crested the hill ahead. The man she desired was so busy dodging questions and keeping secrets to realize he loved her.

She gave D'Artagnan his head, letting his competitive spirit catch them up to Luke and Monster. By the time she reached the creek, he was spreading a small blanket a few yards from where he'd tied off his mount. "Turkey or roast beef?"

"Either is fine." After securing her mount, she joined Luke on the blanket. Lying on her side, she took in the lush vegetation on the bank, the hum of bees, and the scent of honeysuckle. Her gaze lingered on the man next to her. His skull trim, piercings, and gauges, none were reminiscent of the man she once knew. Those amber eyes, though, they and his heart hadn't changed. "This place has so many happy memories for me. It was my escape."

"What did you have to get away from, princess?"

An old pain ached anew. "Despite outward appearances," she whispered. "My life wasn't perfect. Mom and Dad held me to ridiculous expectations, ones I frequently failed to achieve. Grades, social contacts, appearance…"

"Ignore me." He touched her hand. "I remember some of the crap your folks put you through. Red ribbons were never good enough."

A bitter laugh escaped Julia's lips. "Second place won't do, even in a pursuit my mother didn't approve of. On the other hand, your mother was wonderful to me. Always an encouragement."

“That was her. She’d be so pleased to see you now.”

“Do you think she knew about us?” They’d taken great pains to keep their relationship secret.

He began pulling food from the bag, passing her a sandwich and bottle of water. “She knew.” He didn’t look her way.

But didn’t approve.

“I wondered back then.”

They ate in silence with her beginning to wish she’d chosen another way to celebrate. She hadn’t meant to dredge up old memories, at least not unpleasant ones. Her recollection of the years she spent at the Rockaway farm was colored with the innocence of youth.

“I didn’t mean to darken the mood here.” He turned his attention to her. “When will you begin the expansion?”

She loved that he believed her plans for growth were a foregone conclusion. “The minute Richard’s check clears, I’ll be in touch with the owner of Wolfe Winery.” She hummed with anticipation. “I can’t wait for you to see what’s in my head. It’s going to be fantastic. I want you to have the first bottle out of my vineyard.”

He arched an eyebrow.

“Yeah, right. I guess I got ahead of myself. I forget you’re leaving soon.”

He edged closer to her. “Not because of you, princess. Despite you. You’re the tether that keeps me grounded to this place when I want to fly as far away from here as the earth will let me.”

His words pierced her heart. “Not the farm?”

"I accomplished my goal of buying back my family's home. If it weren't for the tornado, I would have left and never looked back." Pain flashed in his eyes. "I would have avoided you completely."

His words cut her to her soul. "You saying that almost makes me grateful for the storm."

"Almost?" His lips twitched.

"People got hurt. I'd never be happy about that." Would she have been happier if their paths had never intersected? Certainly, without the tornado, her plans wouldn't have suffered a setback. Her mother wouldn't have been injured and her son's life upset. She also would have likely accepted Richard's plan to commingle their personal and business lives. To most in her social sphere, Richard's offer made sense, despite not loving him. Sometimes, she wondered if she even liked him. He'd come along at a point when she'd needed professional help and someone she could trust.

"I'm happy you're back in my life, Luke, even if it's temporary."

His dark gaze raked over her. "I'm not. It took me years to get over you. I feel the echoes of the pain even now. Knowing it will be fresh and raw again fills each moment with dread."

His words reflected her emotions rather than his. She drew a blanket of protection around her soul against the hurt he'd stirred. "You'll find someone else if you let yourself."

"No, never. You've ruined me for any other woman."

Confusion tangled her thoughts. "Then why don't you stay?"

"I've been here too long already."

"What pulls you back to Ohio?" Was there a woman up there despite his assertions to the contrary? Surely only the strongest of draws would pull him back if he had feelings for her as he said. "Never mind. I'm sorry I asked. Let's talk about something pleasant."

He inched closer. "Enough with the words." With a low growl, his lips pressed against hers in a hungry kiss.

She kissed him back, channeling her frustration and desire into that single act. He licked across the seam of her lips, begging entrance. She readily let him in, stroking her tongue along his. Quickly, he took over the kiss, lowering her to the blanket.

"I want you, Julia. Will you let me have you?"

"Yes. Here, now, I want that. I want to be yours." Lust made her voice breathy.

He gazed down at her, his golden eyes darkening. "Only for this moment, my dear. That's all I have to give."

Tears pricked the back of her eyes. Even in this moment of passion, he was planning his escape. She nodded, not trusting herself to speak.

His hands trailed down her body to tug the shirt loose from her jeans. Then his fingers tunneled underneath. The coarseness of his touch set her skin on fire. She arched her back, wanting more.

"I'm glad to see I'm not the only impatient one." He chuckled then shucked out of his jeans.

"It's been too long."

"In reality, yes. But I've made love to you a thousand times in the weeks I've been back and at least a million more in the past decade."

"You were never far from my thoughts. Even…"

"Enough. No more about regrets." His hand trailed down to the button of her jeans.

Buzz… Buzz…

Julia would have ignored any other ringtone. "That's Paul."

Luke rolled off her and began redressing.

She pressed a hand to her chest and drew in a calming breath. "Hello?"

"Where are you?" Her mother's voice pitched with irritation. "Everyone is back at the house, and Paul needs to get back home to his wife."

"Luke and I took the horses for a ride." A twitch developed over her right eye. "Tell Paul he can go. Teresa can keep an eye on Aiden if you're not up to it."

Her mother let out an impatient huff. "You can't just disappear like this. You have responsibilities."

"Obviously, I haven't disappeared if you found me, and I'm the last person you need to lecture about accountability. I simply took an hour for myself." Her gaze cut to Luke's bare back. An hour she'd never forget.

"That's beside the point. I had a call from Richard Pierce. You and I need to have a conversation."

Damn him.

She massaged the space between her brows. "I'll be back shortly."

Julia turned to Luke who'd shuttered all the raw emotions previously visible. "Duty calls." She stood and began redressing while he collected the picnic.

"It's probably for the best." The emotionless words better fit a missed appointment than interrupted lovemaking.

Pain lanced through her heart. Two could play the

no-big-deal game. "Afraid reality won't measure up?"

Luke turned on her, taking her into his arms. "Never." He brushed back a wayward curl from her face. "I shouldn't have let things get as far as they did. I'm sorry." He released her then walked over to Monster and untied her.

"I'm not."

"I'll race you back." He nudged his horse and took off.

Julia glanced over their idyllic spot one last time before mounting D'Artagnan. Giving the horse his head, they surpassed Luke and his mount in seconds. As they crested the hill, and the house and stable came in sight, she slowed the horse to a walk. With each step they took, responsibility settled more firmly on her shoulders.

At the barn, Luke took the reins from her. "I'll take him from here."

She studied her boy who seemed pleased to have bested the other horse and sufficiently fatigued to tolerate someone other than her tending to his needs. "Behave yourself." She patted the stallion's rump and turned toward the house.

Lovely smile, gentle voice, spine of steel.

"You know what's best for you and your business, Julia. Don't let your mother bully you into something you don't want."

She turned toward him. "Have you met my mother?"

The corner of his mouth turned up. "A time or two. I've also seen you make a mason cry."

She bloomed under his praise. "I'm off. Wish me luck."

“You don’t need it.”

No, I need you.

Julia pushed that thought to the corner. She wanted Luke, but keeping secrets was more important to him than keeping her. As she crossed the space between the barn and the house, she muttered to herself, “But, I don’t need my mother’s approval.” On her business choices or Luke. “Because trying to please her is like trying to fill a bucket with a hole in it.

Chapter Thirteen

D'Artagnan snorted as his mistress walked way. "I hear you, buddy." Her long tresses blew in the breeze as her impossibly long legs took her up the path toward her family. Luke longed to call her back, to take her in his arms once more. The desire to smooth away her problems grew to rival the need to steal her away again.

Her ex met her on the porch before she could shuck out of her riding boots. "You're not the only one she's got to take care of."

The statement applied to him as much as it did the horse. He had no right to feel greedy when he had no business wanting her in the first place.

Julia glance his way.

Luke held his breath, hoping they wouldn't come down for a visit, especially if the ex joined them. Not much got passed the guy and there was no way Luke could hide his feelings toward Julia as raw as they were. He brought the horses inside the barn, curried them down, before turning them out into the smaller pasture to graze.

After cleaning the tack, he reached for the key to his apartment. The door gave way as he touched it. Had he forgotten to lock it this morning? Not likely, prison had taught him caution and suspicion. He toed off his boots before taking the stairs one silent foot at a time. At the entrance to the room, he eased his head around the opening. Laptop and tablet were where he'd left them…almost. His attention zeroed in on a sofa cushion that wasn't right. One of the kitchen drawers wasn't closed all the way, either. "Amateur."

Tension coiled in his gut as he moved deeper into the room. In the corner where he'd set up a small office, the invoices weren't in the careful stack he'd left them. "Who'd been in his space?"

Paul had opportunity, motivation, but plundering wasn't in his character. Going on their one recent encounter, if Julia's ex wanted info he'd straight up ask for it. By contrast, the subtle shift of papers and slightly askew furniture screamed Richie Rich.

"Asshole." The fact only documents pertaining to the Highlands job were in the apartment eased a little of his worry. "He must be getting desperate to hold on to Julia." Men like Pierce thought their money exempted them from the rules, and when cornered they didn't hesitate to stoop to dirty dealing.

Luke walked to the window overlooking the house. He envisioned Julia and her family gathered around the table. After she'd tucked Aiden in for the night, she'd have an honest conversation with Mrs. Chandler.

If only I could do the same with her.

He held to that thought for only a second. Even if his mother hadn't made him promise not to tell, he wouldn't want Julia to know what happened after his family left Magnolia Valley. He liked how she had looked at him without fear as others did. Loved that she wanted him and respected his opinion. All that would change if she knew.

Luke stripped out of his clothes and got underneath the shower. He had to get her out of his head. Nothing good could come from acting on their feelings.

"Three more weeks." He just had to fly under Pierce's radar until then.

****

As Julia mounted the first step, Paul rounded the edge of the wraparound porch opposite the barn and parking pad. "Hold up." He lowered his phone from his ear and shoved it in his pocket.

"Why are you standing out in this heat?" Anxiety joined the cocktail of emotions already churning in her stomach.

"I wanted to catch you before you went inside."

"What's wrong?"

He waved away her concern. "Stop worrying so much. Everything's fine." He cocked his head. "But your cheeks are flushed. That must have been some ride."

Her gaze shot to the barn. Did he suspect what was going on between her and Luke? Was he going to dissuade her from the relationship?

She drew in a deep breath and prayed for calm. "Luke and I took the horses out for a ride. After getting the call from Mother, we decided to race back." She grabbed the bootjack from beside the door and lowered to the swing.

"I'm glad to see you taking some time for yourself. You work too hard."

"Don't start." She wagged a finger at him. "Listen, there'll be enough nagging once I get inside."

Paul nodded toward the house. "Speaking of Helene, fair warning, she's in rare form."

Tossing the first boot to the floor, she rubbed the twitching muscle between her brows. "How much shopping did she do?"

"Not…too… much, mostly clothes for Aiden."

Julia tugged the second boot free, dropped it to the floor next to its mate, and studied her ex-husband. They'd been together long enough for her to know when he was glossing over the truth. "And?"

"I tracked them to Meyer and Berkley. I talked her out of buying a pair of sapphire earrings."

More likely he'd saved Helene from the embarrassment of having her card declined. When her mother refused to stick to a budget, Julia set strict limits on the credit cards she used. "Thanks for running interference."

"I also tried to talk her into staying the night with Michelle and me, but she insisted I bring her back here."

"I appreciate the effort."

He shrugged. "Sorry."

"No worries. I can handle her and your mother."

"You always were good with them." He opened the backdoor for her.

In the mudroom, off the kitchen, she continued their conversation. "They're like children, feed them and keep them occupied, otherwise they get into mischief." She gestured to the kitchen. "You're welcome to stay for supper. I'm grilling steak."

"That sounds good, but I need to get back. I'll just scoot through to the living room to say my goodbyes." On his way through the kitchen, Paul paused and looked over his shoulder. "I know you say you can handle our mothers but you're also under a lot of stress with everything else going on. Don't let them get over on you. You're the judge of what's best for your life—

not those two."

Julia's eyes widened. When did he become so philosophic? The smallest of smiles tugged at her lips. "Thanks for the pep talk. I'll remember that when they start tag-teaming me."

He lifted a hand in goodbye. "You know they will."

Following Paul's departure, Julia grabbed a quick shower. During dinner prep, she also prepared her responses to the moms' relentless campaign to manage her life. By the time she had supper on the table, she was ready for battle. She passed the dish of corn-on-the-cobb to her mother. "How was shopping?"

"Not as nice as it could have been."

"Really? I thought you two went to Phipps."

"We did, and Paul met us for lunch. But then he wouldn't let me buy this darling suit for Aiden. He said, 'the boy needed a suit like a hog needed a sidesaddle.' Can you believe that? Of all things to say to me. Despite my best attempts, he dug in his heels. So, your son is without a new suit for when school starts back."

Julia's attempt at navigating the conversation didn't preclude the straying of her own thoughts. The dining room windows provided a full view of the stables. Light from Luke's apartment captured her imagination. What did he do to fill the hours when he wasn't working? Did he still love reading vintage westerns the way he had in college?

"Have you heard a word I've said?" Her mother tapped her arm.

Julia jolted at being snatched from her ruminations. "Pardon?"

"What's going on down at the barn?"

"Nothing." The rise in pitch gave Julia away.

"Then why do you keep looking down there?"

She waved her hand. "Just wondering how D'Artagnan is doing, that's all."

"Uh-huh. Sure." Her mother took a sip of wine and dabbed the corners of her mouth. "I've been meaning to ask why you didn't invite Richard to supper tonight. I understand you had some small success today."

Julia turned her attention to Aiden to give herself a moment to decide which part of her mother's statement to address first. That "small success" would be what paid for Helene's shopping trip today.

Aiden, if you're finished eating, you can watch some dog videos before bath time.

Her son signed thank you for supper and scrambled from the room. She didn't allow Aiden much screen time, but she also didn't want him to witness what could turn into a contentious conversation between mother and grandmother. When the sounds of puppies yelping came from the next room, Julia turned back to her mother. "Richard has other things to keep him occupied."

"Is everything okay between you two?"

"Of course, Mother, why wouldn't it be?" She'd be damned if she'd discuss the caveat Richard wanted to add to their business arrangement, or that he might pull his financial support if she didn't give into his suggestion for them to become lovers.

"Don't be dense. It's unbecoming."

Teresa rose from her seat. "Why don't I get Aiden ready for bed?" She offered Julia a sympathetic look as she scurried from the room.

Julia let out a breath and began collecting the

dishes. "Contrary to your assessment, I'm quite aware of what you're insinuating. I'm choosing not to argue with you."

"You need to look to your future."

"That's what I've been doing for the past three years, Mother. Once Richard writes me a check, I can begin the expansion. In five years, I'll be debt free, and you'll be able to refurbish Oakton."

"Is that how you see yourself spending the next twenty years?"

It wasn't her ideal. That option lay a few hundred yards away. "It wasn't my first choice, but fate took me in other directions."

"It's not too late to have another child. Richard would make a wonderful father."

"Can we talk about something else?" Julia massaged her temple. "I like working. There's nothing between Richard and me but business."

"That's not the way he sees it."

Her temper flared. "Not because I haven't told him often enough. That's his choice if he wants to see things differently."

"Teresa thinks her Paul is stubborn, but you've got the market cornered on mulishness. That and lunacy. How in the world you could let not one millionaire, but two, slip through your fingers is beyond me?" With that cutting remark, her mother swept from the room.

"I prefer to think of it as tenacity and independence."

Julia sank into one of the dining chairs. By now her mother's barbs shouldn't hurt quite so much.

After cleaning the kitchen, she spent time reading to Aiden. The sweet-scented boy cuddled in her lap acted as a balm for her soul. "As long as you're happy, safe, and fulfilled," she whispered to her son as he drifted off to sleep. "I will support anything you choose to do with your life."

Once she had Aiden tucked in for the night, she returned to the living room. It didn't surprise her to find Teresa watching TV alone. A thwarted Helene was a churlish Helene. "If you don't mind being on your own, I think I'll sit on the porch for a while."

"She means well."

"That's what I keep telling myself."

Julia closed the door behind her and sank to the swing. Lightning bugs flickered in the night and cicadas called to potential mates. She'd done her best to help her mother see the situation from her point of view. For Helene, financial security, or the illusion thereof, ranked higher than love. That outlook simply wouldn't work for her, no matter the consequence.

One of the horses whinnied from the barn. Another answered the call. Julia turned her thoughts to Luke and his darkened windows. Did the nighttime stirring of the animals disturb his sleep or had he grown accustomed to the noise? She had a thousand things she needed to do and pondering his sleeping habits wasn't one of them. Yet, she couldn't bring herself to return inside. For all that Highlands gave her purpose, something was missing from her life. She wanted to be loved and love in return. Not courted for her looks and hostess skills.

D'Artagnan's nicker carried on the night air. She rose from the swing and stepped on to the grass. Padding down the dark path, she told herself she was only going to check on him. After feeding her boy a couple sugar cubes, she peeked in on the other horses.

Luke had topped off each water bucket and laid down fresh sawdust. Once again, his tender heart shown through the armor he wore.

Her gaze shot to the tack room. She crossed to it, heart pounding as she opened the door. Passing the saddles and bridles to Luke's apartment stairs, she told herself to have a little more pride. Or at least some self-preservation.

Luke made it abundantly clear that while he found her desirable, he didn't want a relationship. She knocked on the door. Would he answer? Would he turn her away? She had to give it one more chance. If things went the way she feared, at least she could say she'd done all she could. After this, she'd quit trying to make him love her. She couldn't give up, not without one more attempt.

It didn't even matter that Luke had secrets. She had her own.

He opened the door, still drawing on a pair of shorts. "What's wrong?"

She wanted to ask if that was how he saw her—someone whose problems he needed to fix. She hadn't come down to the stables to pick a fight.

"I ahh…" Her words trailed off at the sight of his bare chest. She looked around hoping a legitimate excuse would present itself.

Luke pulled her over the threshold and into his arms. His mouth was on hers, seeking. He raked his fingers through her hair, gently tugging it free from the ponytail. "I must be dreaming. You're all I've thought about. Surely, I've conjured you up."

Julia buried her face in the crook of his neck. "If it is a dream then let's don't wake up."

His arms banded her waist, hauling her deeper into the large room. “Why are you here, princess?”

“To be with you.”

His pupils dilated. “I can’t tell you how many times I almost came up to the house.”

She pressed a kiss to his pec. “Be glad you didn’t.”

“You should know by now I’ll defend you against anyone, even your family.”

“The only thing I need is you. Make love to me, Luke, just this once. I know you can’t make promises. I’m not asking for any.”

He kicked the door closed and carried her to his bed. There, he laid her atop the rumpled covers. After pulling off his shorts, he joined her. His hand caressed the length of her before moving to the hem of her shirt. He drew it over her head and tossed it to the floor. “So very beautiful.”

“You make me feel that way.” Her hand trailed down to his hips.

He stopped her before she could act on her thoughts. “Tonight, is about pleasuring you.” Fire sparked in his eyes. “And acting on the fantasies I’ve had all these years. Will you let me do that?”

How could she say no? “Absolutely, and this time nothing short of a fire is going to stop us.”

Luke threw his head back and laughed. “I heard that.” His mirth darkened, replaced with lust as she shimmied out of the rest of her clothes.

Blood heated her cheeks. She scurried to join him under the covers. All her life she’d been admired for her appearance, but something about his gaze made her feel as if he glimpsed her soul. Did he like what he saw despite her shortcomings? Tucking the dark thoughts into the corner, Julia snuggled in close to his hard body. She'd allow nothing to ruin their time together, not even her insecurities.

When she reached for his hard length again, he stopped her. "Later. I have something that needs attending to first. Something that requires my undivided attention."

"So, making love to me is a job?" A fissure of insecurity opened. "Another task to take care of?"

"I would like nothing better than to spend the rest of my life in your service. Giving you pleasure is the only payment I require."

Oh, God. Her eyes fluttered closed. If only there could be more than this one time. Emotion bubbled up, rushing to her lips. This time she managed to clamp down on the words that spoiled their first time together.

****

Luke traced his finger across Julia's cheek. Watching her breathe was the most glorious, intriguing pursuit, and he'd never tire of it. But, even in sleep, her mind still worked. Her brows creased, and her lips moved. He longed to kiss away whatever worry disturbed her slumber.

As he leaned down, she jolted awake. Her gaze shot around the room. "How long have I been asleep?" She threw back the covers. "What time is it?"

He caught her hand to prevent her from leaving. "It's only been fifteen minutes. You can stay a bit longer." Though a thousand years wouldn't be long enough.

"I have to get back to the house." But she allowed him to tug her back into bed.

"In a bit. First, tell me what you were dreaming

about."

"I dreamed another tornado came and destroyed the vineyard. I was trying to catch the grapes."

He choked back a laugh. "Knowing you, you would try to take on a tornado." What he didn't understand was the force behind her drive to take on the world. "I don't get you. Women like you aren't driven to succeed. They want husbands and spa days."

She jerked up the covers. "What do you mean, women like me?"

He held up a hand. "That was badly worded. I didn't mean to offend you." He brushed back a strand of hair. "The fault lies with me."

"You better believe it does."

"I said, I was sorry. Will you let me finish? I'd like to dig myself out of this hole if you please."

She made a circle with her hand indicating he could go ahead.

"You don't fit into the stereotype I placed you in. I thought all southern ladies of good breeding wanted nothing more than a life of ease. And yet, you seem to court hard work like it was a Hermes purse."

"Like I tell my mother, work isn't a four-letter word."

"You're right; it's not. But you seem to be driven by some terrible force."

"I am." Her gaze fluttered around the room, as if she was deciding whether to confide in him. "It's fear."

"Of what, not having money?"

"That's part of it."

"Your ex-husband would never let his son, or you go without."

"That's not the point. I want things in my own

right, not because someone is looking after me. My life should be more than an extension of someone else's. I also want to set an example for Aiden. He's going to have a lot of people tell him he can't do things because of his hearing impairment. I want him to see me succeed when people thought I couldn't."

"Those are all noble causes." Somehow, he fell a little more in love with her if that was even possible. "Can I tell you something?"

"Sure, but be prepared if it's another stupid statement, I won't be responsible for my actions."

He trailed a finger across her bare shoulder. "You can stop worrying about the legacy you'll leave Aiden. If you never accomplish another thing, he has a mother he can be proud of."

Her face glowed with his praise, making him wish he'd offered it more. "That's kind of you to say, but there's so much more I need to accomplish. I want Highlands to be synonymous with luxury and success." She held up a hand. "Before you ask, yes, money is important. People depend on me to take care of them. Not just my employees, who obviously can find other work. My mother depends on me and my business for every penny she spends and doesn't even know it."

"How's that? Your family is one of the oldest and wealthiest in Atlanta."

"We've got the old part, not so much the wealthy, anymore. My father died suddenly right after Aiden was born." She paused. "As terrible as losing him was, the circumstances of his death had a profound effect on my mother and me. She stubbornly clings to the way her life was when she was a young girl and her every whim could be entertained."

Luke let out a breath. "I wish I could fix this for you."

"Listening is enough. I didn't tell you this because I expected you to reciprocate. I may not know everything that's happened to you in the past, but I know *you*, the man you've become. That's enough." She touched his face. "Say you'll come back to visit me. I know your life isn't here now, but I don't want you to disappear on me again. At least promise me you'll say goodbye before you leave."

His pulse thrummed in his ears. He'd lost her once, and fate had seen fit to give him a second chance. "What if—" He swallowed hard. "What if I didn't go back to Ohio? How would you feel about me staying here in Magnolia Valley?"

"Let me show you."

Her answer led to more lovemaking, and when he finally let her slip from his bed, he resolved to do whatever it took to do right by her this time around.

Chapter Fourteen

Early the next morning, Luke peered out his apartment window in time to see Julia drive away. Their conversation last night deserved a follow up, but first he wanted to get his sister's input on the idea that had kept him awake all night.

"How's my nephew?"

"Jake's good. Growing like a weed. He's looking forward to visiting his uncle's farm, if you're going to still be down there for a couple more weeks."

Luke had the perfect mare for the boy to ride. "I am. He can come whenever he wants. I'd like you to visit as well if you can get off work. If you can't make it during the summer, Thanksgiving or Christmas would work as well."

"You're staying at Rockaway Farm? When did that happen?"

"My change of plans is a recent development. I'm considering making Magnolia Valley my home base." More like the center of his world with Julia and Aiden there.

"Does this change of plans have something to do with *the princess*?"

"She's changed, Yvonne." His sister's use of the nickname irritated like a dull razor across his skin. Did he sound as condescending when he used it? He cringed. At first, certainly, but as he grew to know Julia better the sobriquet changed into a term of endearment for the regal woman who'd grown from a spoiled southern belle to a woman of worth and substance. "People often grow up over a decade or two, especially when life throws them a few difficulties. If you gave her a chance, you might find you like her."

Yvonne let out a huff that carried the distance from her home in Kansas. "I very much doubt that, brother mine."

"Well, I love her, so you better set your mind to a few changes." With the force of his declaration, came the realization. "I'm completely in love with her." He sank to his unmade bed, grabbing the pillow where Julia had rested her head.

"Oh, Luke, no. How did you let that happen again? You know it could never work with you two."

He brought it to his nose, breathing in the sweet scent of her perfume. "You're wrong. It can."

Silence filled the air. "You're not … You're not considering telling her, are you?"

"I am." Certainty settled his anxious mind. It was the right thing to do. "Have you ever told?"

"Never even considered it."

Like him, his sister carried a heavy burden. "Not even that guy you were engaged to a couple years ago?"

"That was part of our problem. He knew I was keeping something from him. In the end…"

"I know what you mean. Julia knows something bad happened that August. She's asked me to confide in her several times. Things have changed now, and she's willing to stay in the dark." But what impact would that have on their future?

"Mom made us swear to keep Russell's death a

secret for a reason."

"Yeah, her pride." He loved his mother and had kept the promise all these years to honor her. "It's our secret, and I'm tired of keeping it. I plan to tell Julia everything that happened, but I wanted to check with you first."

"Go ahead. She's nothing to me. I'm telling you, though; this won't have the happy ending you're expecting."

Making love to Julia hadn't turned him into a member of the optimist club. "Maybe, but I can't start my future with Julia off this way."

"I hope she's worthy of you."

"I'll let you know how it goes."

He hung up from the call certain of his actions but undecided about his approach. "I murdered a man with a baseball bat," was a statement he needed to ease into. He had faith in her. She'd understand why he'd taken a life and the guilt he would always bear. With no secrets between them, they could move forward. Maybe even give Aiden a brother or sister.

As he headed to Highlands to supervise the finishing touches on the main ballroom, he let optimism have a toehold on his heart. Maybe even ex-cons got a second chance.

****

Julia entered the main ballroom looking for her new assistant, Phylicia. When she found Luke alone, her plans changed. She eased beside him and tugged the tablet free from his hand. "Come to dinner tonight."

He wrapped her in his arms, making her forget all the niggling details of Highlands's approaching reopening. "I'm not sure that's a good idea. I don't think I can keep my hands off you." He proved his declaration by caressing her from shoulder to hip.

"That's okay within limits." She sank into his embrace.

His eyes narrowed. "You want us to go public?"

"Of course. Why wouldn't I?"

"What will Helene and Teresa say?"

"That you're charming, and I'm lucky to have you in my life. That we deserve this second chance."

"I'm not sure the grand dames will agree with that sentiment."

Julia ran her hand over his pecs, feeling the hard plane of muscle beneath her palm. "They like you. They find your French accent charming."

"Perhaps as a dinner guest. As your lover, not so much."

"They just need to get used to the idea." Or not. Their opinion carried no weight. Aiden adored Luke, signed his name a dozen times a day. That was all the approval she needed. "Come to dinner. We'll hold hands. You'll play with Aiden, and they'll see how wonderful you are. Just like I do." She stood on tiptoes to kiss him.

He took her by the shoulders. "There's something I need to tell you first." His jaw ticked.

"There's nothing you could say to change my mind about you." All that mattered were the promises he'd made last night. Luke was staying, she could stop fearing she'd wake up one morning to find he'd disappeared again.

"I hope that's true, my darling. I really pray that's true."

Anxiety sent pinpricks across her skin. "You're

making me nervous. What's wrong? Are you changing your mind about us? You know all that social standing stuff isn't important to me. That's my mother's hang up, not mine."

He touched her cheek. "I know, and it makes me love you even more. Your disclosure about her father and his estate got me thinking."

"I told you that you didn't have to tell me anything." She clutched his shirt, desperate to make him stop.

He kissed her fingers as she reached to cover his mouth. "I know, but it's important you hear this."

Fear had her pacing in a circle. Why had she pushed him to share the secrets of his past? The ballroom door opened, and her assistant peeked inside—an interruption when they needed to be alone. "Be right there, Phylicia."

She returned her attention to Luke. "I'll meet you at your apartment at noon." Privacy was what they needed. Lots and lots of privacy. Whatever he had to tell her could be worked through if everyone else in the world would leave them alone for two seconds. "I have a meeting with Richard in a little while. I'll come to your place afterward."

His frown deepened. "No, I'll come to you."

"You know you've got nothing to worry about with Richard." But did she? He'd yet to sign the papers to complete their financial agreement.

"I wish I could agree."

"You've got nothing to be jealous about, but I kind of like that you are. Not very progressive of me, is it."

The corner of his mouth turned up. "You bring out the Neanderthal in me. Every time the little prick's around, I want to throw you over my shoulder and bellow, "Mine!"

"Now that's a mental image." She chuckled. "That's something I might want to revisit."

He drew her in for a kiss, one that curled her toes and made her eyes roll up in the back of her head. "Now get going. We've both got work to do and you're waking up Little Luke. I've got to go over your punch list with the subcontractors, and I'd just as soon not do it with him at attention."

****

After Julia left, Luke returned to the work at hand. With anger his only emotion for so long, experiencing joy, love, and peace had his mind playing catch-up with his heart. His love for Julia had been so much easier to deal with when he thought her out of reach. She'd bridged the distance of their social standing and his past. If only he didn't screw it up.

Richard Pierce's southern drawl echoed from the lobby on the other side of the ballroom doors. God, he despised the prick. If only there was some way to get rid of the financial investor and still have Julia achieve her dreams of expanding her business.

"There you are." Richard entered the room, closing the doors behind him. "Your gang wasn't certain where their leader was."

"Julia's expecting you. She left for her office a few minutes ago."

The man's thin lips slit into a smile. "I'll catch up with her shortly. It's you I want to see at present."

Tension shot through Luke's body. He crossed his arms. "I'm right here."

"I'm hoping you can help me with a situation." He

drew closer, his smile growing more predatory with each step.

At least those years in prison had served some purpose. He'd faced more deadly adversaries than the seersucker-wearing man before him. "I doubt it. I can't imagine a scenario in which I could benefit you in any way." Luke might as well let the fucker know he was wise to the plans he had for Julia. "If you want me to convince her to go to bed with you, you've come to the wrong guy. That's her decision, and she's chosen *me*."

The verbal jab hit its mark, but Richie Rich recovered quickly. "That's a place you may occupy for the moment. I assure you, once she's gotten over her nostalgia, she'll come to think of what's best for her and her business."

"There's more to life than the bottom dollar."

"So, you say. Highlands is important to Julia. I'm looking out for her best interest. I have connections and social standing. What can you offer?"

Luke leaned in, causing the other man to step back. "Love. An emotion you're incapable of understanding. She loves me and I her."

"How poetic, but beside that worthless sentiment, what can you give her? I want what's best for her. Do you want the same?"

He warred with his temper that wanted to show Pierce exactly the lengths he'd go to prove his love for her. "I'd give her my life if necessary."

The smile returned to the man's face. "I'm glad to hear that. It will make things much easier on her. Perhaps she can come out of this with minimal detriment."

Luke narrowed his brows. "What the hell are you

talking about? I'd never hurt Julia."

"Then you'll see why you need to leave. I'm what's best for her. I can offer her the connections she needs to make Highlands a national success."

"She can achieve that on her own if you'd get out of her way."

"How do you think Julia would feel if she knew your secret? Would she feel the same about you?"

"I'm planning to tell her."

"It's good to hear you're finally being honest. She should know that she's sleeping with a murderer."

He wasn't wrong when he suspected someone had broken into his apartment. "That was you."

"Just doing my due diligence. I believe in knowing my competition as well as I know my friends. I sensed there was a reason your family left Magnolia Valley all those years ago. I just never imagined you'd be such an easy rival to dismiss. Man slaughter—got you five years. How was Holman Correctional Facility?"

Luke tamped down on the urge to take the guy by the throat. "If you know all that, you know the circumstances behind my actions."

Pierce cocked an eyebrow. "I believe in protecting what's mine, and I'm not prone to squeamishness. However, would Julia feel the same once I show her the photographs my private investigator obtained? They paint a very graphic image of a very violent man."

"It was either him or my sister. Russell Abbott was beating her to death." Luke clenched his fists as the memory of that night flooded back. "There was no contest. I'll explain it all to Julia. I'm sure she'd agree."

Richard nodded. "Perhaps. I can certainly see now why you kept this from her. How would she feel about having a killer around her son? You've proven your propensity toward violence with the way you handled that barn manager."

"I've never struck anyone for my own benefit. I was protecting my sister back then and a defenseless animal that day in the barn."

"Given Julia's family history, I'm not sure how she'd feel about bringing a murderer home."

"What the hell are you talking about?"

"Her Father. Didn't she tell you how he died?"

"No, just that it was sudden."

"It certainly was. I was well-acquainted with Albert Chandler. Such a brilliant mind and generous philanthropist. His violet death was a senseless tragedy. It was a wrong place, wrong time thing, but that mattered little in the end. A good man died that day. At the time, it devastated Julia, threw her whole family into chaos. She confided in me once, her father's death contributed to the breakup of her first marriage." Pierce *tsked* as he shook his head. "And Mrs. Chandler, poor woman, the shock alone of discovering her daughter was sleeping with a murderer would probably *kill* her."

"I had no idea." Nausea swept over him. "She just said her father died suddenly."

"You can see how this will never work. Save her from having to make the hard choice. I know she believes she's in love, but only because she doesn't know you the way I do. She puts on a brave front, only showing the world the confident woman, she wants to be. On the inside, she's still a daddy's girl wanting someone to buffer her from life's harsh truths."

"That's bullshit. She's the toughest woman I know."

"Now, but you didn't see her after her father's death. The way he died shook her to her core. Can you risk that she could withstand another blow?"

"I would never hurt her, or any woman. I was trying to save my sister."

"Will Julia understand that?" He cocked his head. "Do you want to see the look of fear on her face?"

Every muscle in Luke's body tensed. That had been the reason he hadn't told her to begin with. He couldn't risk hurting her again. But leaving would do just that.

"I'll leave you to think about your choices. I'm hoping you'll make the one best for Julia." Pierce trotted from the room like a racehorse that'd just crossed the finish line.

Luke collapsed into a nearby chair and buried his head in his hands. A large part of him wanted to race to Julia, fall at her feet, and beg her to listen. He simply couldn't add to the pain she and her family had already experienced. He'd cut off his right arm before he'd see fear darken her beautiful face. As lovely as she was, she struggled with anxiety and the eating issues that it brought on. One more blow, another burden to shoulder, might be her undoing.

If given the opportunity to re-do that fateful night, he wouldn't change a thing. It was either Yvonne or her abuser. He sacrificed Russell's life in fact, and his own in essence, to save Yvonne and his unborn nephew.

Even with that, he realized with what Julia and her family had gone through, she wouldn't want to be with a man who'd taken another's life. He tossed the tablet onto a table. After a few words to his foreman, Luke climbed into his truck. A quick pit stop at the apartment for his bike, and he was on the road. Breaking the promise not to leave without a goodbye would cause her pain but not nearly as much as the truth.

Chapter Fifteen

Knock, knock

Julia took a deep breath and mentally prepared for her meeting with Richard.

Lovely smile, gentle voice, spine of steel.

"Come in."

Richard entered her office, pulling the door closed behind him. A somber expression replaced his usual confident smile. "Hello, there. Thank you for letting me invade your already busy day."

She motioned him to one of the newly reupholstered chairs across from her desk, buying time to regroup from this unexpected change of his persona. Arrogance, she expected. Bravado, a given. The subdued man who sat before her, what did she do with him?

"Is everything okay?" Was this how he'd terminate their business dealings?

"I'm afraid not." He placed his monogramed briefcase in his lap. "You see, I ran into Topher at the club a few days ago…"

Her heart sped up. Was her neighbor backing out of their verbal agreement to sell Wolfe Winery? "Go on." *Spit it out, for crying out loud!*

"I only pursued the gossip for the sake of Aiden."

At the mention of her son, Julia's hackles stood up. "Get to the point, Richard."

He removed several sheets of paper and placed them atop the case. "Of course, but first I want you to know it grieves my heart to do this."

Heart? She wasn't sure he had one. As she looked him over, she wished, not for the first time, there'd been other finance options available.

Perhaps the country club gossip he'd heard concerned her mother's financial situation. Though the impact to Aiden would be minimal due to Paul's business acumen. Surely, he didn't think to play some role in her son's life. The words, his behavior, the papers in his hand, nothing added up.

She massaged her temple. "Richard, I really don't have the time or the emotional energy for this. If this is about the other day, I've said everything there is to discuss. Unless you can accept a friendship on the terms I outlined, we're done."

"I've given what you said due consideration." He sat up straighter. "While it's not what I'd like, I concede it's your prerogative to feel as you do. I hope we can move beyond my bad behavior and begin anew."

"You really mean that?" Julia narrowed her eyes. "You understand my feelings toward you will not change."

"We'll be spending a great deal of time together in the future. I'm hoping we can be friends as well as business partners."

One thing she'd learned was not to burn bridges unnecessarily. She couldn't afford to create an enemy in their small circle of friends. "Certainly. I'd like that."

"I'm glad." He let out a sigh. "Now to my odious task."

She tensed, waiting for him to undo all the good will he'd created. "Go ahead."

He looked down at his hands. "I'm not sure how best to broach the subject. The last thing I want to do is interfere in your personal life. You've made it abundantly clear my opinion isn't valued in that respect."

Ah, Luke.

Why had it taken her so long to guess the topic he was dancing around? She spared little time connecting the dots on the gossip trail. Now that she and Luke were finally on the same page, she wanted the whole world to know they were together. "If this has something to do with Luke, then you'd be correct. I love him, and there's nothing you can say to change my mind about him."

"For your sake, I hope that's true. I'd hate to think his past would tear you two apart again."

Her heart hammered. What did he know? "It won't because I won't let it. I've told him that what happened before doesn't matter. We're moving forward with a clean slate."

"I wonder, how your family will feel about you bringing a murderer into their midst?"

Julia's ears rang. Surely, she'd heard wrong. Luke wouldn't lay a hand on someone, much less take a life. She slammed her fists on her desks as she stood. "That's a damned lie."

"I'm afraid not. According to the report I obtained from the private investigator I hired, a Luke Chevalier was arrested twelve years ago for killing a man named, Russell Abbott. Luke was subsequently tried, convicted, and served five years of a ten-year sentence." He pushed the report across the desk.

With trembling hands, she took the paper containing a typed report and newspaper clippings from an Alabama newspaper. She sank back to her chair. Her gaze scanned the words, absorbing the horrors they detailed. Had the man she loved truly taken a baseball bat to someone?

That explained his sudden disappearance and his family's evasive answers concerning his whereabouts. Was he even capable of that level of violence? He'd been so gentle with her, treated her mother deferentially and Aiden—he'd learned ASL to communicate with him.

The memory of the day they'd transported the horses to his farm flamed in her mind's eyes. He'd had the barn manager by the throat. What would he have done if she hadn't intervened?

Only the grip she had on her chair kept her from falling over. "I had no idea."

Richard crossed to her side of the desk, placing a hand on her shoulder. "It pains me to be the one to bring you this terrible information. All along something about him had me worried. A man who alters his appearance, the tattoos, the piercings, does so for a reason."

Julia weaved in her seat. "I need a moment to process this. Please leave."

"I take no joy in being right." He stroked her head, sending her further down the black hole of nausea. "I'd give anything to be wrong about him."

She held up a hand, stopping him from putting an arm around her. "Stop. I've heard enough. Go."

"Not until I'm sure you're okay."

Lovely smile, lovely— Reciting her mantra wouldn't help her out of this situation. She willed the churning in her stomach to calm and smoothed her expression. "I'm fine." She rose on legs as steady as ribbons then motioned him toward the door. "If you'll excuse me, I have work that needs my attention."

"Sure. I'll be spending the night at my condo in town, but I'm just a phone call away."

As the door closed behind him, she lost the battle with the nausea. Barely making it to the powder room off her office, she sunk to her knees and emptied her stomach. After lying on the cold marble floor, she let the tears flow. How could Luke have kept such a monumental secret from her—not only then but now? Her heart ached for him. For his family. For her.

Weeping solves nothing.

Julia pushed off the floor then gripping the edge of the sink, she brushed her teeth and wiped the smudges of mascara from underneath her eyes. "We just need to talk things out. I'm sure Luke can fill in the details that led up to that night."

Her hands shook as she pulled up his number from the contacts on her phone. Richard had painted a black and white picture of the events. In her experience, limited though it might be, rarely were things as clearly defined. Luke deserved an opportunity to fill in the details as much as she deserved to hear them.

Holding her breath, she pushed the button on her phone to connect the call. The sound of Luke's voice mail plunged her back a dozen years.

A missed nightly call.

Two days of worry.

Waiting.

Followed by evasive answers from his mother.

The first week of classes she must have called his phone a hundred times, leaving progressively more desperate messages. By the end of the week, fear had her by the throat. Skipping Friday classes, she'd driven from Sweet Briar to Rockaway Farm to find the place deserted. Horses relocated. People vanished.

The beep at the end of his recorded message pulled her back to the present. "Luke." She swallowed past the lump in her throat. "Call me as soon as you get this message." What she needed was to look into his golden eyes and see the truth as he explained himself.

Julia stormed out of her office, her thoughts a tangled mess of anger, fear, and panic. This couldn't be happening to them. They'd fought hard for their second chance. They'd earned it. She could barely string two thoughts together, but even with all that, she knew what Richard had told her was true. Yet, she clung to a thread of hope somehow Luke could explain things further. She left her office in a full run.

His crew was putting the final touches on the lobby. The repairs to Highlands would be completed by the end of the week. She barely noticed the marble floor and new wall sconces as she rushed up to one of Luke's crew. "Billy, where's Luke?"

Something flashed across the guy's face. He lowered the paintbrush and turned to her. "I'm not sure where he went, Ms. Wilkes. He left out of here a little while ago."

"Did he say where he was going or when he'd be back?" A sense of urgency gripped her. It was enough to make her want to take the guy by the shoulders and shake the truth out of him.

Billy studied the ground. “Didn’t say where he was going. Just left instructions with the foreman.”

She let out a breath. “Where is he?”

Billy was all too happy to point out Jerry’s location, and she took off in the foreman’s direction. “What instructions did Luke give you before he left?” She bypassed niceties and preliminaries, as a sickening sense of déjà vu washed over her.

Jerry scrubbed the back of his neck. “We’re to finish up with the lighting and painting touchups. Then I’m to oversee as the landscapers do their thing.”

Her stomach tightened. Anxiety danced along her skin. Those were punch list items she and Luke planned to go over together this week. “He’s not coming back, is he?”

“No, ma’am. But he said I should see to it you were satisfied before we pulled up stakes.”

It was one thing to imagine history repeating itself, another to learn the truth was worse than she’d feared. Now she understood why he’d left. “I see.” She choked back tears then straightened her shoulders. “Thank you. I’ll touch base with you later.”

Pity softened the man’s eyes. “I’m sorry, Ms. Wilkes. If it’s any consolation, it must have been something important to make him leave in such a hurry. He looked right tore up.”

A momentary spark of hope flared. Maybe he wasn’t running off again. Perhaps, something had come up with his sister. She flinched at her own selfishness that she’d wish misfortune on another. “Thank you. I’ll see if I can reach him by phone.” She walked off, heading back to her office for her keys and purse. With any luck, she could catch up with him at the farm.

As she covered the two miles that separated her land from his, she tried to piece together the sequence of the day's events. The morning started off wonderfully. She and Luke had turned a corner. Then Richard arrived with his news and false concern. He'd been to see Luke before coming to her with his information. The realization had her gripping the steering wheel as if it was his scrawny neck. Julia would deal with him and the chaos he'd unleashed as soon as she caught up with Luke.

She pulled off the highway and on to the gravel drive leading up to the house. In the pasture, D'Artagnan's head came up as she drove past. She scanned the area underneath the oak tree where they parked their cars. Teresa's oversized SUV blocked the view where Luke usually parked his motorcycle. As Julia drew nearer, her hopes raised when she caught sight of the truck he used at the construction site. She exited the car and walked over to it. His toolbox rested in the bed. The cooler he used as a lunch box sat on the seat.

Julia placed a hand on the still-warm hood. He had to be at his apartment. Had to be. Had to be.

She turned toward the stables, a spark of hope still flickering inside her. All they needed was a good, honest conversation to straighten things out.

The door to the house opened, halting her. Her mother stepped out onto the porch. "You're home early. I wasn't expecting you until tonight. We haven't eaten lunch. Shall I set a place for you?"

"No, thank you, Mother." She gazed up at the apartment window overlooking the small paddock. "I need to speak to Luke then I'm headed back to the hotel."

"He's not there. Aiden and I were feeding carrots to one of the ponies when he came in. He went up to his apartment for a moment then left out of here on his motorcycle."

"Did you speak to him? How did he seem?" Her voice rose as she fought the urge to jump in her car and chase after him. Where would she begin to look for him? She didn't have his address in Ohio, not even the name of the town where he lived. His sister, Yvonne? Only that, a name.

"As far as speaking, he didn't say anything to me. He did come over to Aiden and signed something, but I couldn't make out what it was. It seemed to upset him though." She gestured inside the house. "Teresa's trying to distract him by reading to him."

Julia's concern shifted. "I'll come inside and see if I can calm him down." She found her son on Teresa's lap signing, *Luke*.

Tears welled in Julia's eyes.

Hi, sweetheart. She knelt to brush a lock of blond hair out of the boy's face. *Grand M says you're having a rough day.*

Luke gone, pumpkin gone, He signed over and over.

No amount of self-control could stem the flow of tears as she watched her son struggle to make sense of his loss. Between the trauma of being caught in the tornado, the death of his beloved pony, and a move, no wonder the boy was having a hard time. Julia pulled her son into her lap and the two of them rocked and mourned their loss together.

"You go eat your lunch," she said to her former

mother-in-law. "Aiden and I have some talking to do."

The two of them climbed the stairs to the boy's room and following a difficult conversation, he finally settled down to play with his stuffed dogs. With a final look over her shoulder, Julia went back downstairs.

"I'm going down to the stables for a few moments."

The statement drew the attention of both women who were in the dining room wrapping glasses in tissue paper in preparation for their move back to Atlanta. "We'll be fine. Take your time," they called one after the other.

Repairs on Teresa's house wouldn't be complete for several months, but she'd invited Helene to join her at a condo in Buckhead Paul leased for his mother. She suspected this was his way of helping without seeming to do so.

Julia's steps lacked the urgency they'd had an hour ago. Even knowing she'd missed his departure, she couldn't keep from checking. She found the large room tidy as always, except for the coffee mugs she'd place in the sink that morning. Had it been only this morning that she'd been so full of hope? She scanned his desk area, noting the invoices and permit documents for Highlands neatly stacked on the side of the desk. He'd taken the laptop.

Next, she made her way to the bedroom area. Atop the neatly made bed, a single piece of paper caught her attention. She snatched it up, anxious to find some plausible explanation that would make the nightmare bearable.

Princess,

I know I promised to tell you before I left. In this,

and many other areas, I have failed. As you move forward to a future filled with success, I hope you'll eventually come to look back on our time together with some level of fondness. I know I will treasure it always and will ever remain your faithful cavalier.

Luke

She sank down on the bed, trying to make sense of the note. Was she losing something in the translation? She expected him to explain his leaving, defend his actions, or cast recriminations on Richard, in some way address the new tornado tearing through their lives. Had he already planned to leave and the conversation he'd had with Richard was simply the catalyst for a departure three months in coming?

For certain, she'd have a sharp conversation with her *friend* soon, but that *tête-à-tête* would keep.

She lay down on a bed still smelling of Luke's aftershave and let the tears flow. Tomorrow would come soon enough and with it a laundry-list of problems for her to face. Then, she'd rise and fake the bravery she needed to slay tomorrow's dragons.

Chapter Sixteen

After returning to Ohio, Luke woke one Saturday to the driving need to hop on his bike. Between the gaping wound from leaving a big part of himself back in Georgia and a niggling anxiety something else was amiss, the walls of his tiny house had begun to shrink. Without any clearly defined destination, he headed south.

He finally ended up at the Mable Creek livestock auction, but not to buy anything. His place wasn't big enough for a dog much less a three-quarter ton horse. The sights and smells reminded him of happier days, recent and long ago. Sitting up high and some distance away from the men in overalls and Amish farmers dressed in plain black, he settled in to watch the stream of cattle, horses, and smaller herd animals. He'd always loved coming to the big stockyard in Calhoun, Georgia, joining his father from the time he was big enough to climb inside the cab of the farm truck. After prison, he hadn't wanted the reminder. Now, the past seemed like a warm friend with whom to spend countless hours. Why not when nothing of interest lay in his future?

A handler led a gorgeous Arabian into the ring and the bidding began. Julia would love this filly. The animal held her head erect, scanning the galley as if she were challenging buyers to take her on. Seconds after the winner was announced, a pre-teen girl raced to the edge of the ring. All manner of jumping and arm-flailing ensued. A man followed, likely the girl's father, and attempted to quiet her as the animal was led off.

The best-day-ever scenario prompted an idea. He left his seat and joined the crowd down front. Several quarter horses and some goats later, one of the handlers led a possibility into the ring. An announcer gave the particulars of the pony. The six-year-old gelding looked good, old enough to be past the frisky stage and young enough for Aiden to grow up with the animal.

When the bidding commenced, his hand shot into the air. As the amount increased, so did his pulse and not because of the cost. He wanted it for Aiden…and him. When the dark thoughts threatened to take over, he needed images of the boy trotting around the ring with his mom looking on to think about.

Luke suppressed the urge to fist pump when he finally prevailed. Amid making payment and arranging shipment to Georgia, his phone rang. The caller ID had him stepping away from the noisy arena.

"Jake, buddy, what's up? Is your mom okay?" He talked to the boy regularly but only after speaking to his sister.

"She's fine, I think. I found her crying earlier. I thought maybe you could cheer her up. I tried giving her one of my chocolate bars."

Yvonne Yvhid her battle with depression well, affecting a cheery persona only the most observant saw through. Medication and therapy brought the effects of her abuser to mostly manageable levels. She was also determined her son would enjoy a normal life. If Jake caught her at a weak moment, things must be bad.

"Put her on and I'll see what I can do. First,

though, you did good. Don't worry about your mom."

A few moments passed. "Luke?" Her voice floated across, paper thin. "Sorry, I didn't hear your call. Jake said you wanted to talk to me."

"I do, and the reason you didn't hear was because Jake called me."

She didn't immediately respond.

"You still there, Yvonne?"

"I guess I'm not hiding it as well as I thought."

"Talk to me. Did you schedule a session with Dr. Willoughby?"

"No, I'll be better tomorrow. I get like this every year on this date."

Shit! That's what had been rattling around in the back of his brain. He'd been so busy trying to get from one moment to the next, he'd forgotten the anniversary. Today was August seventeenth; the murder happened exactly twelve years ago. "I'm sorry. I should have remembered. I've just been all up in my head about stuff."

"How did it go with Julia? Did you tell her?"

"No." He toyed with what to tell his sister. The last thing she needed was more guilt. "I learned something that made me rethink things."

"Are you still in Georgia?"

"I'm back in Ohio. For good."

"Oh, that's too bad."

"Enough about me. I want you to schedule an appointment with Dr. Willoughby."

Silence filled the connection before she spoke again. "How often do you think about what happened?"

"Not as much as I used to." As time passed, he could go whole weeks and not think about the blood on his hands. Sometimes it would be a month or two before some little event or a comment would send him back to that night. “You?”

“I thought I’d gotten passed it. I like my new job. Jake is doing great in middle school. Then I looked at the calendar.” Her voice broke. “This is all my fault. If I’d left him, made better choices, Mom and Dad would still be alive. You’d be a vet with your own practice. You and Julia would be together.”

He grieved for his sister. “You don’t know that. Dad’s ticker was bad before then. Breast cancer runs in Mom’s family. And Julia and I were never a given. We had issues before. This isn’t your fault. I want you to understand that.”

“It’s not yours, either. Russell’s death or how it played out with the princess.”

“I know that.” Most of the time. He couldn’t help reexamining the events leading up to him taking a baseball bat to the asshole’s head.

“I would be dead if it weren’t for you.”

And Jake as well since she’d been seven months pregnant with him at the time. As it was, the beating sent her into labor, and the boy had been born two months premature. “I’d do it all over again. Every minute of it. Russell was never going to stop.”

“I know. I can’t help wishing things were different. Jake asked about his father a couple weeks ago.”

Luke’s heart seized. “What did you tell him?”

“Just that he died before he was born. Don’t worry, I’m never going to tell him. I don’t want that image in his head.”

“I agree.”

Yvonne needed him, and he had to do something

other than pine for Julia. "I have an idea. Why don't I come for a visit? Jake's birthday is in a couple days. I could do some man stuff with him."

She gave a tired laugh. "That would be great. See you soon, brother mine."

****

"Chef wants to know if we're going to offer a full menu on our overnight room service." Phylicia read from a page-long list of questions coming from various newly hired members of staff. This was after Julia had met with the heads of each department. Chef Aaron, a recent graduate from a culinary school in Atlanta, had blown her away with his interview dishes. Unfortunately, some of his practical skills weren't as dazzling. She hoped what the twenty-five-year-old lacked in experience, he made up for in quick learning.

She turned from her computer. "Tell him, 'absolutely. We give our guests the best of everything even if it means cooking a filet mignon at three o'clock in the morning.'"

She rubbed at the permanent twitch that had developed over her right brow. For someone who loved cutting tags off the latest fashion and thought new-car-smell should be turned into a perfume, she longed for the comfort of her old office furniture and the familiarity of having people around her who knew how she liked things done. None of this was the fault of the new staff. They were good people, professionals. It took time to build a team.

Phylicia glanced at the tablet she clutched in her hand. "I think that's all, Ms. Wilkes. I'll get on these rights away."

When the door closed behind the girl, Julia let out a

breath. Her hand inched closer to her phone. She longed to punch in Rachel's number, not just because her friend was an excellent second-in-command and could run a wedding weekend like troop movement. Mostly, Julia needed someone to talk her through the pain and loneliness keeping her awake at night and convince her one more text wasn't going to get Luke to respond. The Moms attempted to distract her with news from the country club set. Paul just looked at her like he wanted to say something but didn't want to set off the waterworks. The few members of her pre-tornado team tiptoed around like she was a cross between a rumbling volcano and a wet ginger cat.

Her mother breezed into her office, dressed in a lovely pale-yellow suit. "I rode up with Paul, Michelle, and Aiden. Let's all go to lunch. I want to celebrate my new freedom." Her leg had healed enough to where she only needed a cane to get around. Having regained a measure of independence, she and Teresa were the first to leave the farmhouse, moving into her friend's new condo. "I heard there's a new bistro in town featuring farm-to-table salads."

The thoughts of food turned her stomach. "I can't leave now Mother. We'll have to eat in the staff dining room. Highlands has another wedding this weekend and the out-of-town guests will check in tomorrow. Following that, one of the businesses in Alpharetta booked a conference for next Monday and Tuesday."

Before Luke's departure, Julia planned to have a grand reopening event—invite family and friends from Atlanta in addition to locals. Afterward, putting one foot in front of the other was as much as she could manage. Especially now that she planned to turn down

Richard's offer to invest in her business.

He couldn't possibly believe she'd want him as a business partner after he hired a private investigator to investigate Luke's past.

Her dream of purchasing Wolfe Winery might be slipping beyond her grasp, but at least one thing had gone well. Aiden transitioned back to their suite at Highlands like he'd never left.

Too bad she couldn't say the same. Back at Rockaway Farm, she couldn't stand looking out at Luke's apartment over the stables. Yet, moving back to the hotel felt like she'd given up. Maybe she had. Julia closed the door on expanding her business. Without Richard's investment, purchasing Wolfe Winery was as likely to happen as hearing from Luke.

Her mother planted a fist on her hip. "Surely your staff can manage so you can take an hour for lunch."

"No, they can't." She let out a sigh. "Besides being unfamiliar with how I like things run, we've got a planning meeting to discuss the Winter Festival during the holidays."

Helene let out a huff. "We'll meet you in the dining room in ten minutes then, work or no work."

Later, her office door burst open. "I'm just finishing up now, Mother."

Aiden ran headlong into Julia. The boy's hands flew so fast she couldn't decipher what he was trying to tell her. She caught her son in her arms.

Slow down, sweetheart. Let momma give you a hug.

She breathed in the scent of baby shampoo that never failed to make her womb clench with longing.

What fun things did you, Daddy, and Michelle do

this weekend?

Aiden formed the letter "H" with his right hand then placed his thumb on his right temple, bent and unbent his first two fingers a couple times, creating the sign for horse.

Did you go riding?

Surely not, though there were stables near Teresa's house they could have used.

Aiden emphatically repeated the sign then tugged on Julia's arm.

She chuckled. *Okay. I'll follow you.*

Paul entered her office, breathing hard. "There's something outside Aiden wants to show you."

"I got that. What's going on?"

At the end of the hallway, Aiden took off. She chased after, only catching up with him at the rear door leading to the employee parking lot.

At the north end of the new stables sat a small horse trailer. As they neared, Julia picked out movement inside.

She shot a glance at Paul. "Did you buy him a pony?"

He shook his head. "Not me. We pulled in behind the trailer. I thought you did it. I made Aiden come up to the hotel to get you before they unloaded it."

"It wasn't me." Though she wished she had. After the new stable had been constructed, she'd moved D'Artagnan and his herd back home. It was time to consider Pumpkin's successor.

Julia peeked inside the trailer, saw a lovely Connemara, and then turned to the driver. "Where did this animal come from?"

The man opened his palms. "All I know, lady, is I

picked him up in Ohio and was given this address."

Luke. She covered her mouth. Surely it had to be him. Tears welled.

Paul cocked an eyebrow. "You get it figured out?"

She nodded. "I think Luke sent this for Aiden."

"Why would he do that?"

Her heart ached. "I'm not sure." Was he sending a message?

"You going to keep it?"

Was it something to remember him by or a gesture of kindness from one horse lover to another? Most likely it was the only closure she'd get, a token to remind both she and Aiden of happier days. "Absolutely." She glanced down at Aiden who was rigid with anticipation. "Do you want to be the one to tell him he can't have it?"

Paul cracked a smile. "Not for a million dollars."

After arranging to have her mother spend the afternoon availing herself of Highlands's spa, Julia turned her attention to Aiden's gift. She inspected the pony, finding him an excellent example of the breed. He stood perfectly still as she tacked him and then circled the ring on the lunge line, moving from one gate to the next.

Finally, an impatient Aiden could ride his new mount. With Julia holding the bridle, the boy rounded the ring.

I don't think he has a name, sweetheart, so you get to be the one to decide what we'll call him. Be thinking of something special.

The boy nodded, and his brows knitted. Holding the reins cut his method of communication, but no doubt, the wheels were turning in Aiden's head.

You could give him a name that describes what he looks like or the way he acts. It could be something funny, cute, or even a people name.

The six-year-old leaned down and hugged the pony, brushing his mane with tender strokes. He lay atop the animal for several seconds before sitting upright.

Her heart seized. How had she not recognized how much her son missed Pumpkin? Aiden rode the other horses readily enough, but nothing measured up to that one special mount. Or replaced his fellow horse lover. Aiden missed Luke and was still signing his name daily. Should she tell her son who'd gifted him the pony?

Better not, otherwise she might be calling Luke from the pasture for the next thirty years.

Chapter Seventeen

Julia trailed behind Aiden as his dad carried the exhausted and dusty boy from the stables.

You can go back to check on Buttermilk before bed.

She turned to Michelle who'd, along with Paul, stayed to see Aiden ride. "Since we skipped lunch, why don't y'all stay for an early dinner."

Michelle hooked her arm through Paul's as they entered the hotel's rear entrance. "We don't want to put you to any trouble, but I'd love to see the hotel now that the restoration is complete."

"I'll give you the grand tour myself." Her vision for the remodel had come to fruition. A sleeker, more polished Highlands replaced the English country design of the pre-tornado hotel. Thanks to Luke's crew, the place looked pristine. Every light fixture glimmered, the walls shone in pearl-gray, and the carpet cushioned beneath their feet. "And dinner is no trouble at all. We can eat on the terrace or there's room enough for the five of us at the table in my suite." She gestured to the kitchen door before leading them further down one of the staff hallways to the private suite where she and Aiden lived. "Chef Aaron keeps my fridge stocked with meals for me to reheat."

Paul barked a laugh. "I'd stay just to see you actually put food in her mouth."

Just as her ire flared, he let out a pained grunt.

"Damn woman, you've got a bony elbow."

"And I sharpen it every night for such occasions as this." Michelle nodded to Julia. "Sorry about that. I'm trying to teach him to keep some of his thoughts on the inside where they belong."

A smile tugged at Julia's lips. "You're doing a better job than I did."

"But she's so thin." He gestured the length of her. "A stiff wind would blow her away."

Michelle narrowed her gaze like the elementary school teacher had plans for Paul's recess.

Chuckling, Julia unlocked her door. "He's been through this with me before, so I guess he's earned a say. I'm making myself eat twelve-hundred calories a day."

Paul jerked a nod. "It's just that Helene mentioned how much weight you've lost."

Julia scanned her sitting room for her mother who no doubt intended the comment as a complement. "Did she say if she'd be joining us for dinner?"

"While you were with Aiden and the pony, Mrs. Chandler sent word by one of the staff that she's retired to one of the guest rooms for the evening," Michelle said.

Pushing aside the irritation at the misuse of her employee's time, Julia took her mother's apparent enjoyment of Highlands as a positive sign. Perhaps convincing Helene to live at the hotel full-time might prove easier than expected.

Following a light supper, Paul and Aiden left for the pool. The late summer days warmed the water, making a dip more like a bath than a swim. On the weekend, the resort would be filled with Atlantians up for a quick retreat then as the season progressed, leaf-peepers would keep her and the staff busy. For now, Julia and her family practically had the hotel to themselves, and the other guests weren't using the outdoor pool. As father and son splashed in the shallow end, Michelle and Julia sat in nearby chaise lounges.

Michelle let out a contented sigh. "Paul means well. He can't seem to help himself when it comes to looking after his family."

Julia recalled her reaction to her father's shocking death and all that fell on Paul's shoulders in the aftermath. Her weakness shamed her now. "In the past, I've given him reason to worry." Michelle toyed with the stem of her wine glass. "I know it's none of my business, but how are you doing after..?"

No need to pretend Julia didn't know what Michelle was talking about. Between Teresa and Helene, she didn't have much chance at keeping her relationship with Luke secret.

"Not great." But at least she hadn't fallen apart as she had in the past. Facing down her dragons didn't stop the ache in her heart, though. "I keep thinking it will get better." Perspective was what she needed—a friend to speak some words of wisdom. With Rachel in South Georgia, her source for good, old-fashioned home truth was miles away and busy with her own life. "Do you mind...?" Was this even a subject she could broach with the wife of her ex?

Michelle turned in Julia's direction and cocked an eyebrow.

"Could I ask you a personal question?"

"Absolutely."

Julia drew in a breath and let the words flow from

her lips. "Have you ever been in a situation like mine, where a relationship ended suddenly?"

Sympathy colored the woman's face. "Not like you've experienced, no. Paul never disappeared on me, but we broke up for a while. I don't mind telling you, it was pretty terrible."

"You must have found some way to cope. How'd you get out of bed in the morning? If it weren't for Aiden, I'd stay under the covers for the next twenty years." She turned in her seat to face Michelle.

"I was a mess for several weeks."

"But it got better, right?" *Please, say it gets better.*

"Truth?"

She didn't want to hear the truth if it meant this pain in her chest wasn't going away, but she nodded anyway. If this was something she was going to have to live with, she needed to get some coping strategies. Luke's first departure paled in comparison to the vacuum he'd left in her life this time around.

"The pain dulled after a while, but it never went away."

"I was hoping this time would be different. Luke and I have a past, see, before I met Paul. One day, he and his family left town. Just disappeared. I didn't learn why until just recently."

"Didn't you reach out to them?"

"I did. Weeks after leaving messages, his mother finally called me back."

"What did she say?"

"Just that Luke didn't want to see me anymore."

"That's a very unchivalrous way of handling a breakup, letting your mom do your dirty work."

"It wasn't until a little while ago that I learned he

wasn't in the position to contact me. It's still not my story to tell. His family has always wanted to keep what happened private."

"But all this pain you're feeling is about what happened this time."

Julia sat back, putting some space between her and Michelle. "I shouldn't be doing this to you. I'm sure you never signed on to be your husband's ex-wife's therapist."

The other woman reached across the distance to take Julia's hand. "We're family. You can tell me anything, and I promise to listen." She met her gaze. "I also won't be discussing what you say with anyone else. I know how the Wilkes clan is."

"Part of the problem is I'm mad at myself. When he came back into my life, I thought it was our second chance. He kept telling me it was temporary, that he was only here long enough to help me put Highlands back together. I didn't want to believe him."

"You and I are optimists. We want to believe things will work out the way we want them to."

"Even when the truth is right there in front of us. My father always said an indicator of future performance is past behavior. I should have known. I did get him to promise to tell me goodbye when it came time for him to leave this time."

"And he just left? Again?"

"Yes." Julia brushed the tears from her cheeks. "That's what makes me so angry. He just assumed I couldn't handle the truth about his past or a goodbye."

"Maybe it was he who couldn't handle saying goodbye. Did you ever think of that?"

"No," she squeaked. She hadn't looked at it from

his perspective at all. He'd been in so much pain all those years. He'd suffered and carried so much guilt. "I would have understood. I'm stronger than I look."

"You're right." Michelle looked around at the gardens and pool area. "You've accomplished a great deal and endured what would have crushed others."

"He should have given me a chance." She clenched her fist, pain morphing into anger.

"Have you tried contacting him? Phone, text, email?"

She nodded. "A couple calls and texts that first day. After I read the letter he left, I stopped. It was obvious he didn't want to talk to me in person. A few words scribbled on a sheet of paper is all the closure I'm ever going to get. All because he believes I'm a princess who couldn't handle un-pleasantries."

"Everyone deserves the truth, even when it's painful to hear. Even when it alters their perceptions."

"Amen to that."

The conversation acted as a balm—until a disturbing thought occurred to her.

I'm doing the same thing to Mother.

Protecting Helene from the truth about their finances and covering up the circumstances of her father's death. All because it might fracture her view of the world. "I'm guilty of coddling my mother for similar reasons. But not anymore. The time has come for me to treat her the way I want to be treated—whether she likes it or not."

****

"How did you sleep last night, Mother?" Julia motioned for one of the waiters to remove their breakfast dishes from the iron table where they were enjoying their meal on the lower terrace. Aiden, who'd woken Julia at dawn signing, *Buttermilk,* had eaten a few bites before scampering down to the stables for his first lesson on the new pony.

Helene dabbed the corners of her mouth. "I rested well. The mattress was quite comfortable."

So far, so good.

Julia scheduled a meeting with Richard at his offices in Atlanta for later that morning, which meant she'd have back-to-back come-to-Jesus-meetings today. "And how was your spa experience yesterday?"

"Lovely." Her breathy drawl stretched the two-syllable word to three. "I feel like Queen Elizabeth and Scarlett O'Hara all rolled into one."

"I'm glad you enjoyed yourself." She reached in her pocket and slid a small box across the table. "I have a gift for you."

Her mother clasped her hands to her breast. "These must be those earrings I wanted bank in the spring. That's the reason you said I couldn't have them. You wanted to surprise me."

Julia shuttered her eyes and prayed for patience. Her mother was nothing if not determined. "I'm afraid not."

Helene crossed her arms. "That was a rude trick to make me think you'd gotten me those sapphires. You knew I had my heart set on them."

"That wasn't my intention." Julia's heart sank even as her frustration mounted. Her first mistake had been reusing an old jewelry gift box. *I should have known better.* She'd hoped to make her plan appear to be a luxurious gift instead of the option-less arrangement it was. She nudged the box closer. "I put a great deal of thought into this present. It is something I hope will bring you many more years' enjoyment than jewelry."

Helene cut her eyes at her daughter. "I can't imagine anything that would bring me more pleasure than those earrings, at least not something that could fit inside a box this size."

"Just open it."

After tearing off the giftwrap and prying open the lid, Helene took one look and tossed the box onto the table. "What is that?"

"It's a keycard to your new suite. I want you to come live with Aiden and me here at Highlands."

Pfft. "Why would I do that?" Helene raised her chin. "My home is Oakton. Always has been and always will be. Members of my family have been living there since before Sherman. It is my duty to preserve it for posterity."

The knot in Julia's stomach tightened. The mention of heritage, duty, or white after Labor Day often led to fits of temper. "At lease come look at it. The interior decorator designed it specifically for you. She used your favorite colors."

Her mother let out another huff. "Fine. Let's see this Taj Mahal."

Julia took her mother's elbow and steered them back to the main entrance. She hoped another view of the beautiful lobby with its marble floor and lovely European-inspired fountain would remind her mother of the posh surroundings. "It's right next door to mine so you can see your grandson whenever you like." Julia unlocked the door and swept it open. "Ta-da. Isn't it gorgeous?"

They stepped inside. "The designer took her

inspiration from Architectural Digest's piece on Kensington Palace. You have a galley kitchen. Although you need not ever use it since you have twenty-four-hour room service." She walked to the common wall between their two suites and tapped an oak panel door. "This leads to my sitting room, so I'll never be far."

Helene ran her hand over the silk settee. "It's all perfectly lovely, my dear. Your taste has always been impeccable. You get that from me." She shook her head. "But this is not my home. I don't mind coming for the occasional visit, but as soon as renovations to Oakton are complete, I'll return there."

Julia swallowed hard. What if her mother couldn't handle the change?

Everyone deserves the truth, even when it's painful to hear.

Michelle's words echoed in her ears. "Have a seat. We need to talk."

"What's wrong? Is it the windows? The restorer swore to me he could get authentic replacement glass."

"No, it's not that." Where did she even begin? This conversation should have happened years ago when she first discovered the state of their finances. Or before perhaps. When her father finally succeeded in spending the money that had taken generations of Chandlers and Ansleys to amass.

"We've got bigger issues than that. We don't live in the era of huge mansions and dozens of servants. Most people, even the ones we know, don't want to keep up an estate as large as Oakton. I've arranged with the Atlanta Historical Preservation Association to purchase the house and two acres of grounds. They want to open some of the rooms for tours and use others as a learning center. The remaining three acres will be sold off to private individuals."

Helene's eyes bulged. Her mouth opened and closed. "You can't—" She took to her feet. "You can't do this to me. I won't allow it."

Julia took a deep breath. "You have no say. Daddy left me as executor of his estate and I'm the trustee for your trust."

Her mother clenched her fist. "If he were alive today, he'd never stand for it."

"I'm very sorry." Julia kept her voice calm, though her insides were anything but. "We're broke. The only reason I could afford the repairs that are being done now, was because the contractor was willing to take what the insurance paid. I have no money for Oakton's upkeep. Or yours. You run through fifty-thousand dollars a month."

Helene kicked up her chin. "What did you do with my money? It all went into this damned hotel of yours."

The accusation cut her to the core. "I haven't touched a dime of your money. I took the settlement from my divorce to do the first round of renovations. In fact, Highlands had been keeping Oakton afloat before the tornado."

"I…I don't understand?" She sank back to the sofa. "*What* happened to it?"

Julia had hoped to keep her father out of the conversation. As old-fashioned as it seemed, speaking ill of the dead didn't sit well with her. "I don't think going into specifics will help. What's done is done. Daddy made some poor choices resulting in the loss of nearly all our investments, property, and cash."

Helene wagged a boney finger at Julia. "I won't have you dragging your father's good name through the muck. He was a good man. Except for a few dalliances, he was the perfect husband."

Dalliances! Her jaw dropped. That's what her mother called having multiple mistresses, an illegitimate child, and dying of a heart attack in his lover's bed? "You knew?"

Fire flashed in the woman's eyes. "I saw everything and spoke of nothing. In my day, wives didn't stand in judgement of their husbands."

"So, you know about—"

Helene cut her off. "No—don't utter that woman's name in my presence. Nor will we discuss the circumstances of your father's passing."

"Okay. I'll respect that."

She turned her thoughts to the matter at hand. "As of yesterday, you have less than twenty-thousand in the bank. That should last you until the end of the month at the rate you burn through money."

Her mother's bottom lip quivered. "What about the yacht and the place in Palm Springs?"

Guilt weighed on her chest. She should have never kept these things from her mother. Mostly, she'd hoped to spare her the pain and humiliation, but she'd also wanted to avoid witnessing Helene's world crumbling around her. "I sold the yacht last year and the beach house this past winter."

"My jewels and the antiques?"

"Those are yours. I won't touch them."

"Does Paul know what you've done?" She brought a hand to her mouth. "And Teresa, does she know?" Tears trickled down her face.

"She knows nothing. Although I imagine she suspects something because she called offering to buy those damned earrings for you."

Her eyes grew wide. "You didn't let her, did you? I'd rather die than think it was anything more than a misunderstanding."

"I told her that you changed your mind about them."

"Oh, thank God. Why hasn't Paul helped you?"

She didn't even want to go into the fact it wasn't his job to bail her family out of its financial woes. That concept was as foreign to Helene Chandler as cutting coupons. "He's offered many times. I turned him down."

"Don't you care about your heritage—" Her voice broke. "Or preserving the legacy of your family?"

"The dead don't impress me, and I don't care about the opinions of most of the living."

"That's abundantly clear given some of the things you've done." Helene lifted her chin. "What about Aiden? Don't you care about him?"

It was her turn to climb on the proverbial high horse. She narrowed her eyes. "I'll chalk that comment up to you being overwrought. Aiden is well cared for and you know that."

"What does Richard have to say about all this? Surely, there is something he could do?"

"I'm ending my relationship with him. He's proven himself untrustworthy."

Her mother's mouth opened.

Julia raised her hand. "It's not up for discussion."

All the air seemed to escape from her mother. "There's no other way to save Oakton?"

"The Preservation Association is a way to do just that and allow people from all over the world to enjoy it."

"I guess I now know how Ashley felt in *Gone With the Wind.* My kind of world no longer exists." She broke down in quiet sobs.

Julia let her mother enjoy her moment of melodrama and self-pity without pointing out they lived better than most. Helene had been protected by everyone who'd ever been a part of her life. She was unequipped to handle difficulty.

Her mother choked back tears to ask, "What will people think? How will I ever face the country club again?"

"You can simply tell them you gave Oakton to the A.H.P.A. They've agreed to keep the terms of the sale private. You'll be more popular than ever."

"That's right." She sniffled. "Mary Ellen Bradford's always bragging about how her family donated that Chagall to the High Museum."

Julia patted her mother's knee. "Look at you seeing the bright side of things. We Chandler women are tougher than people give us credit for."

There was still the matter of Helene's monthly spending and the country club dues she could no longer afford. That would keep for another time. Or several times, as it was unlikely her mother would easily take to economizing.

"I'll leave you to get settled." She kissed her mother's cheek. "I've got to head downtown. Feel free to contact Phylicia if you need anything."

"That's fine, dear." Helene waved her away. "I'm just going to call Teresa and bring her up to date on my lodgings." Under her breath she added. "Though I'll be damned if she'll ever learn the circumstances."

"Sounds good, Mother." At least a dozen other topics deserved coverage before the two could move forward in emotional and financial stability—not that Helene would ever consent to hear more from Julia about her father's love child.

Counting the conversation with her mother as a mark in the win column, she left for her meeting with Richard. Tenderness and flattery resulted in détente if not an actual victory with her mother.

Richard Pierce would not receive the kid-glove treatment.

Chapter Eighteen

Julia entered the mirrored elevator primed for her appointment with Richard. Ever since she'd learned he'd hired a private investigator to dig up Luke's past, her head swam with hundreds of sharply pointed words. Words she'd rehearsed dozens of times. In the end, it seemed best to use as few of those as possible, offering the man no avenue to pursue or arguments to brook.

Given your lack of respect for my private life and the boundaries you agreed to, I no longer believe it is in my best interest to continue our association—either professional or personal.

Her aspiration of purchasing Wolfe Winery and expanding her business couldn't be realized. Then again, her hopes of building a life with Luke hadn't materialized either.

As the doors opened onto the thirty-fourth floor of Tower Place, her momentum stalled. A glass and chrome door emblazoned with Pierce Holdings, LLC slowed her steps.

His turf.

Perhaps it would have been better to have the meeting at Highlands where she reigned. "Too late to change now."

Besides, she wanted the option to leave if he wouldn't take no for an answer, something difficult to do in her own office.

Muttering her mantra under her breath, she breached the doors and approached the very blonde, very buxom woman sitting behind a desk. “Ms. Wilkes to see Mr. Pierce. I have an appointment.”

“Right this way.” The receptionist crossed from behind the desk and led Julia deeper into the office. “They’re just getting started.”

They?

She’d expected Richard to try some last-ditched tactic to continue their association. Couldn’t be her mother, Julia had left her back in Magnolia Valley, and Paul wouldn’t interferer, at least not in an ambush meeting. The receptionist opened the office door.

Instead of sitting behind his desk, he was leaning over the front adjusting a laptop. As she entered he turned and flashed a smile. “Right on time, my dear. We were just beginning to go over the contract.”

As she stepped further into the office, the owner of Wolfe Winery came into view. “Topher? I wasn’t informed you’d be here.” Her stomach twisted.

So, this was Richard’s plan.

The man rose and accepted the hand she offered. “Mr. Pierce contacted me two days ago, so we could sign the papers for you to take ownership of the winery.”

The same day she called for this meeting. She’d bet her best pair of shoes he’d initiated the call within the hour.

He tapped his laptop. “One stroke of the keyboard and the bank transfer is complete. The money for your venture will be in your account.” The corner of his mouth turned up. “Just think, this time next year you could be hosting wine tastings with your own label.”

God, she could see it. Thought of little else for months. Guests would begin with vineyard tours. They'd visit the cellar where her vintner would produce the best varieties of merlots and zinfandels Georgia's soil could create. Afterward they could enjoy more wine with dinner back at Highlands.

Her dreams were literally at Richard's fingertips. The speech she'd practiced refused to launch from her lips.

"With my guidance, Julia dear, you'll be giving Chateau Elan serious competition. Together, who knows what *we* can accomplish."

Richard's words washed over her like cold February rain. With his money came an expectation of a romantic involvement as surely as falling in love with Luke paired with heartbreak.

She squared her shoulders, chastising herself for entertaining temptation. After what he did to Luke, his trampling over the boundaries she'd set. Did he think she was some brainless bimbo he could manipulate? Obviously, he did. He probably had a spreadsheet outlining each step of his plan.

Her temper rose.

Liar, manipulator, sneaky-bastard—

A string of more colorful words replaced her carefully worded speech. The jerk probably had an engagement ring in the desk drawer and champagne on ice.

"Mr. Pierce, you seemed to have had a lapse of memory regarding our relationship." Her words flowed sweetly and without a trace of the anger burning a hole in her stomach. As much as she'd relish blasting Richard, she wouldn't embarrass Topher to do it.

Which was probably Richard's motivation. Knowing manners trumped a good tongue lashing in the Good Southern Girls' Handbook.

She turned to her neighbor, choosing to address him instead of the man who'd only twist every word like the narcissist he was. "I apologize for the inconvenience of having you come to Atlanta needlessly. I'm not sure if word reached you at the country club, but mother donated Oakton to the Atlanta Historical Preservation Association. Maintaining her estate was in large part the motivation behind my desire to purchase your property. Recently, events have come to pass which have prompted me to revise my goals, and unfortunately purchasing your property no longer fits into my new plans."

"This is most unexpected." Topher raked a hand over his balding head. "I've made retirement plans contingent on selling the winery. Cristobel booked us on a cruise. She purchased a home in Tampa."

Her heart went out to him. "I'm most sincerely sorry, Topher." She cut her eyes at Richard. "Certain contingencies of accepting Mr. Pierce's investment make it impossible for me to continue the association. Perhaps another buyer can be found. As sad as it makes me, I'm afraid I will not be Wolfe Winery's next owner."

Richard slammed the laptop closed. "You're being completely ridiculous, Julia, and overreacting about a trifling." His pale skin turned puce and drops of spittle left his lips as he stuttered. "Our kind belong together. I did you a favor exposing that thug for what he is. You should be falling down on your knees and thanking me."

Her palm itched. The guy deserved a good punch in that smart mouth of his. Luke was right, though. Violence solved nothing, and her words weren't going to change Richard's mind.

"Gentlemen, my decision is immovable." She turned on her heels and trotted up the hallway as fast as her shaking legs could take her. All the way down to the parking deck she fumed. She'd been robbed of her chance to cut the slippery shyster down to size.

As she hit Peachtree Road, her phone rang. Paul's voice came over the car's system. "Did you pull the trigger?"

"Yes." A murderous vision popped into her brain. "But not the way I wanted to."

"So, you were right. Pierce saw what was coming and had a countermove."

"Absolutely. In the end it didn't matter what he tried, I wouldn't have gone into business with him."

"Given what you told me, I don't blame you." He let out a breath. "I wish you'd let me give you the financing or at least help you find another capital investor."

"I appreciate the offer. Purchasing the winery was more than a professional dream, it symbolized independence. The new-and-improved Julia. Now, my priorities have changed. Maybe some homeostasis is in order."

"It's Chevalier who's done that." Paul growled. "He's another one I'd like to get alone for a few minutes."

She wouldn't mind the opportunity either. Julia chuckled for the first time in ages. "Thanks. I'm coming to realize tying things up nicely or expressing anger with people isn't in the cards for me."

"So, what is?"

"Making peace with the way things turned out."

"I could throw some platitudes at you if you want. Look on the bright side, you've got your health, make some lemonade, or some shit like that."

"You can stop now. I get it." She laughed again. "I'll take a few days to regroup and come up with another angle to draw more business. One that doesn't involve a huge capital investment. Once wedding season winds down, maybe I'll take a vacation."

As ridiculous as it sounded, she pictured driving to Ohio. While she was conjuring up the impossible, she'd miraculously run into Luke and finally get her say with him.

****

"When can I visit your farm in Georgia?"

Luke jerked his attention to his nephew. "What?" Where had that question come from? They'd been discussing baseball, hadn't they? He hadn't been paying much attention to their conversation, letting the boy do all the talking as they built a tree house in the backyard of his sister's house.

"I don't know about that, buddy." He picked up another nail and aimed for the board in front of him. Most likely they'd never make it down to Georgia, not that the property was ever far from his thoughts. An image of Rockaway Farm, and Julia there on it, flashed in his mind.

He missed the nail, hammering his thumb instead. "Dammit." Dropping the tool, he brought the throbbing digit to his mouth.

The boy shrank back to the edge of the lofted

platform as Luke fought to keep the rest of his curses to himself. Pain radiated up his arm. That, along with the blood he tasted, let him know this was more than the typical smashed finger. Thank God, he hadn't been using the nail gun; with his thoughts so tangled he'd have probably put a nail through his head. In the weeks since fleeing Georgia, he hadn't had two brain cells to rub together.

"I'm sorry, Uncle Luke. Mom said I shouldn't ask you so many questions."

"It's okay." He scrubbed the top of the boy's head with his uninjured hand. "This wasn't your fault, and I'm sorry for cursing in front of you."

"It's okay. I hear that one all the time from the kids at school."

"Let's not tell your mother you heard it from me. Speaking of mothers, let's see if she's got something to bandage my finger up."

The two climbed down from the six-foot platform and headed inside.

Yvonne met them on the back porch of her suburban Topeka home. "What happened?"

"Just a minor accident." He held up his hand to examine his pulsating thumb. "Nothing a little ice and a bandage won't fix." And maybe a couple stitches. He really *had* done a number on himself. In more ways than just the damage he'd done to his finger. He'd barely slept more than a few minutes and his gut was a constant brew of emotion. He probably shouldn't operate a spoon much less a hammer.

"I told you it was too dangerous to build that thing." Once they were all inside, she pointed to the sink. "Wash up while I get the first aid kit from the bathroom."

Life after the death of her abuser hadn't been much better for his sister than it had for him. She blamed herself for what happened, and guilt turned her into an overly cautious person, determined not to make any more mistakes. Unfortunately, life was a series of missteps and misconceptions, such as thinking he could escape the consequences of what he'd done. Or that he could build relationship with Julia. Yet, he couldn't bring himself to regret the time he'd spent with her. It had been better than his imagination could have created, right to the point when it went so wrong.

"I build things for a living," he said when Yvonne returned. "Spent a good part of the spring walking across scaffolding three stories in the air. Jake will be fine up there once I get the walls and railing finished," he said addressing her chief objection to the uncle/nephew project.

"I still don't like it." She passed him a square of gauze. "He's going to get hurt."

"Oh, mom." Jake plopped down into a kitchen chair. "No, I'm not. I'll even wear my bike helmet if it'll make you feel any better."

The three of them burst into laughter at the boy's extreme offering, easing the tension in the room.

Yvonne kissed her son's head. "I may take you up on that." She gestured toward the doorway leading into the living room. "Go watch some T.V. while your uncle and I talk."

With the boy in the other room and the television covering their conversation, she sunk to the wooden kitchen chair. "Am I as bad as that?"

Luke took her hand, sandwiching it between his.

"Yes, but who can blame you." She'd been seven months pregnant when Jake's father took a baseball bat to her. The injuries she suffered caused her to go into premature labor. The kid had been born as Luke was being arraigned in a Montgomery County court. "You're doing a good job with him."

"But I worry I'll do the wrong thing, make a bad decision and cause him to get hurt."

"Remember when dad let you help break that Quarter Horse we had?"

"Yeah, I broke my arm."

"Did it make him a bad father?"

"Of course not. Getting hurt from time to time is part of being around horses. Mom and Dad were fantastic parents." She let out a breath. "I could only hope to be that good."

"You are. You just need to relax a little."

Yvonne cocked an eyebrow. "I'd rather concentrate on your issues. What happened up in the treehouse?"

"He asked me to take him to Georgia to see the farm." Luke scraped a palm over his scalp. "It caught me off guard."

"You ready to talk about what happened?"

"Not really. It's for the best that I left. She and I would never have worked out. We're from two different worlds."

"I have half a mind to call her." Yvonne leapt from her seat and paced the area between the table and sink. "I can't believe she couldn't understand the circumstances of Russell's death. She always was a snob." Her words tumbled faster as her agitation increased. "She's probably worried what her rich friends would think."

"I never told her."

She stopped. Turned to face him. "Then *why* did you leave?"

"Someone helped me see it was in her best interest. Her father was murdered in a wrong place/wrong time situation. I didn't think she needed to be reminded of his death every time she looked at me."

Yvonne returned to her seat. "I never liked Julia, but I wouldn't wish that on anyone." She took his hand. "I'm especially sorry for you. You deserve to have someone wonderful in your life."

They fell silent for a few moments. For his part, Luke couldn't help wondering if Julia had moved on? Had Richard finally moved in? There was no doubt in Luke's mind of the fucker's designs for her.

Yvonne broke the silence. "What will you do with the farm?"

"Julia and her family have moved out," he said, repeating the information Jerry passed along. His foreman had also finished up the repairs to Highlands. There was nothing to lure him back to Georgia. "I've already contacted a realtor to find another tenant."

Luke kept expecting the urge to return to Georgia would lessen as time passed. It didn't. In fact, the pull grew stronger as if he were caught by some unseen magnet called unfinished business.

Later that evening as he and Jake sat with their legs dangling off the edge of the completed treehouse, his thoughts were still on Julia.

The boy swatted at a mosquito. "You never did answer my question, Uncle Luke."

"What's that?" Instead of paying attention to Jake as he should have been, he'd been thinking how much

Aiden would enjoy the tree house and imagining Jake and him enjoying a camp out together.

"About going down to Georgia. I want to go. Mom said you two used to ride horses all the time there when you were kids. I want to learn to ride, and I bet she'd let me if we were there."

Luke let out a breath. Guilt added to the already heavy burden on his chest. "I'm sorry, buddy. I can't take you there."

"But you promised."

"I know." Another promise he'd broken, just like his vow to say goodbye to Julia before leaving. The note he'd left on his bed hardly counted. "I'm sorry, but another family will be moving in there soon since I don't plan to live there anymore."

He ruffled the boy's hair. "I'll make it up to you some other way. What say we go to the lake tomorrow? I could teach you to fish."

"Yeah, sure." Jake looked off into the darkness. "Maybe sometime later." He stood then used the rope ladder to lower himself to the ground.

Luke stayed in the treehouse after his nephew went inside. In the darkness, he could think, get his mind wrapped around the events leading up to his departure from Georgia. With each replay, his thoughts returned to the promise he'd made to Julia. And the changes he witnessed in her since college. Richard convinced him she was still too fragile to handle the truth about the murder Luke committed. At the time and given what happened to her father, Luke believed she'd never be able to look at him without fear. While the later might be true, Richard was wrong. Absolutely wrong. Julia possessed depths of strength no one gave her credit for.

Luke owed her his truth and a proper goodbye—as promised. Reaching for his phone, he punched in the number, but couldn't hit the Send button. Julia deserved better than a phone call. He climbed down from the treehouse and entered his sister's house.

"Yvonne, I'm going to head out for a couple days. I've got some unfinished business to tend to."

She lowered her book. "Let me guess—"

"Yes, I'm heading back to Georgia. I won't be long. It'll just be a quick down and back trip. Couple days, tops."

Chapter Twenty

Two months later

A cold autumn wind cut across the pasture as Luke made his way down from Julia's hotel. Her new assistant gave him the same amount of side-eye the old one did as he asked the whereabouts of their boss. In the end, he managed to convince them of the harmlessness of Highland's neighbor. He entered the barn, praying he'd find her alone.

This wasn't his first trip to Georgia, that event having taken place immediately after he left Yvonne's. Learning Julia hadn't purchased Wolfe Winery offered a course of action that might help him make things right with her. Forgiveness and reconciliation were so far down on the list of possibilities, he gave them a mere passing consideration. One thing he'd learned from taking another's life, some actions cannot be undone regardless of the amount of remorse.

He took a moment to appreciate the completed facility. Folks up in Kentucky would nod in appreciation for the place's order, symmetry, and fine appointments. Iron and wood comprised each stall, and a plaque announced the name of each resident. The warm scent of horse, leather, and wood shavings set off an ache in his chest. As long as he lived, he'd associate those with his Julia.

He passed the first stall and one of the mares poked her head out to investigate the intruder. “Hey there, Misty, how’s that foal doing?” He rubbed the mare’s pall, noting her winter coat had started to come in. “It’s about to get cold, isn’t it, girl?”

Just then, Julia stepped from the tack room, drawing his complete attention. She wore jeans and a University of Georgia sweatshirt against the chill of that Saturday morning, and her braided hair now reached the middle of her back. His mouth went dry and his mind blanked. How did he ever think he deserved a woman like her?

Two more stalls to muck out, Aiden, and then we can take our guys out for a ride, she signed.

The boy followed close behind his mother. *Let’s take the Ridge Trail. The leaves are pretty up there.*

Luke’s heart soared as he noted how much Aiden had grown, not just in height but in maturity. The two also seemed to have grown closer if that was possible. They carried on with their conversation as they continued with their chores. He’d have returned another time when he wouldn’t be intruding, but he had a mission to fulfill.

While he was debating how to announce his presence, Aiden looked his way. The young boy tossed aside the bucket and barreled down the hallway, signing his name with every step. Kneeling to his level, he caught him as Aiden leapt into his arms. His fingers moved to spell a different name.

Hold on, buddy. You’re going too fast for me.

Finally, the letters came together to form a word. “Buttermilk?”

Julia folded her arms and met his gaze. “The name

of the pony you gave him."

He stood, setting Aiden on his feet again. Even with her mouth pressed in a firm line and her eyes lit with fire, her beauty struck him nearly dumb. "Oh."

"I hope you realize it's going to take more than a pony to get on *my* good side."

He patted the contents of his pocket, second guessing his offering. What would he do if she rejected it? "I expect so."

She turned to Aiden. *Sweetheart, Mommy and Luke need to talk. I want you to go back to the hotel. Have lunch with Grandmother, and I'll come get you when we're done. We'll still have our ride.*

Luke?

Julia cut her eyes at him. *I'll make sure he says goodbye before he leaves. Don't worry about that.*

The boy hesitated.

I promise. I want to hear all about Buttermilk, Luke signed.

Aiden nodded, but left with the slowest steps he'd seen anyone take outside of Jake being told to do his homework. Once he'd gone, he turned back to Julia. "I've dug a pretty deep hole for myself, but I'm willing to do what it takes to make things right with you." He prayed she'd let him finish the apology he'd practiced and for the strength not to beg for her forgiveness. He certainly didn't deserve it. "Starting with apologizing for breaking my promise. I shouldn't have left out of here the way I did. I was wrong, and I'm sorry."

Her expression softened. "I have some idea of why you might have done so. Richard told me what happened with you twelve years ago. I guess you didn't think I could handle knowing that or the goodbye."

"That's not it at all, princess." He clenched his fist to keep from reaching for her. "Given the circumstances of your father's death, I thought you would be afraid of me. It's never bothered me that others looked at me with fear. But you never did. I couldn't stand it if that changed."

"Hold up a minute." Her eyes narrowed. "What does daddy's heart attack have to do with your leaving?"

"Heart attack? Richard said…" The bastard played him, pulled every string to get Luke out of the way. "He told me your father died violently, and it traumatized you. That you had to be hospitalized afterward. I let him convince me you couldn't take—"

She growled. "That's what I'm so damned mad about. You assumed, like everyone else, that I couldn't handle the truth. So, you just took it upon yourself to decide what was best for me. What I could and could not handle. And you broke the one-and-only promise I asked of you."

"I know."

"I'm not done." She wagged her finger at him. "I thought you were different, that you saw me as I am and not the persona others prescribed to me. If I wanted to be sheltered and pampered, I'd have gone for Richard or had Paul give me the money I needed."

He waited, making certain she had the say she'd earned. Her breath came in little pants. Her cheeks were flaming. Her lips were pressed tightly together.

"About the money." He reached in his jacket and withdrew the deed. "I learned what happened with Wolfe Winery, so I bought it for you. You can do whatever."

"You did what?" Her voice rose an octave.

"I bought it."

"How? Why?"

"I sold Rockaway Farm and used the money to buy the winery because I wanted to show that I believe in you." He thrust the deed in her direction.

"I don't know what to say." She unfolded the papers, reading through them quickly.

"You don't have to say anything. Don't owe me anything. This comes with absolutely no strings or expectations. Not even forgiveness."

Julia's shoulders slumped. "Oh, Luke, I'm not angry. I'm hurt. I appreciate this, but when I refused Richard's investment, I realized I was okay not owning the winery. What I want is a full life surrounded by people who see me as someone they can rely on. Someone to respect."

"That's exactly what you deserve. The property is yours to do with as you will."

"I can't keep it. You've worked too hard. I can't believe you sold your family's farm after working so long to buy it back."

"It was a goal that kept me putting one foot in front of the other. Once I achieved it, and reconnected with you, I wanted other things. I guess I'm like you; material things weren't what I was after. I was trying to make things the way they once were. Crazy, huh?"

"And I want to be completely different from the old Julia."

Luke couldn't resist taking a step closer. "You are, and I wish you every ounce of the happiness you deserve." He brushed a wayward lock of her hair.

"You know what would make me happy?" Tears

turned her blue eyes the color of a clear winter's morning.

"What's that?" If she asked for his very soul, he'd gladly give it to her.

"You."

Julia's gaze raked over Luke. Her whole body trembled. "Having you a permanent part of my life would make me very happy."

"Is that an invitation?" He brushed a thumb across her cheek, his soft touch contrasting with his still-harsh appearance.

"It is, with an emphasis on the permanent. I couldn't take wondering if you were going to disappear again. It wouldn't be fair to me or to Aiden."

"I agree." He opened his palms. "I don't know how to make it right. I've already broken my word."

"I know a way." Her heart thudded, making her lightheaded.

"Name it, and it's yours."

She bit her lip. "Swear it. You'll follow my wishes to the letter."

"With pleasure."

Her hand shook as she held up her finger. "First, I want you to invite your sister and nephew down here. I want to get to know them."

"Done. I'll have them down for Thanksgiving."

She raised her second finger. "Next, I want to make you a partner." She waved the papers he'd handed her. "I can't take this from you anymore than I could take money from Paul. I'll have someone draw up the appropriate documents to make you an equal partner."

"That's too much." He raised his hands and took a step back. "Highlands is worth more than the winery."

Julia narrowed her eyes. “I didn’t ask for your input.” This proposition would be her way or no way. She pointed to the spot on the ground in front of her where he’d stood a moment ago.

He took a step forward. “I graciously accept. I look forward to working with you under whatever parameters you wish to create. No strings. No expectations.”

“Good. I want the two of us to be equals because of my third contingency.” She swallowed past the lump in her throat. What if he said no? “You understand this is an all or nothing proposition. You don’t get to pick and choose. It’s all three or nothing.”

“You haven’t told me the last item. As desperate as I am to do your bidding, it wouldn’t be prudent to commit myself without a clear understanding of my obligations.”

He traced a finger from her shoulder to her hand, then stopped. He was toying with her. Did he guess what she wanted? Did she dare hope he wanted it too? “Marry me.”

Luke scooped her into his arms. “Yes, absolutely. A thousand times yes.”

Elation washed through her. Luke had said yes!

“I can’t believe you still want me. After what I put you through.” He peppered her with kisses, her lips, cheeks, even her eyelids.

“You’re forgiven.” She had to struggle to take a breath from the strength of his embrace. Somehow, she didn’t mind the effort.

“We’ll just have to make up for lost time.”

“I can’t wait,” she said, imagining years of working side-by-side, caring for their horses, raising

Aiden, and perhaps giving the boy a couple siblings.

A small hand tugged on her shirt, and she looked to find Aiden.

Mom?

You little trickster.

Luke met her gaze, telegraphing the same Thank-God-we-kept-things-PG thought she had. *How far did you get before you turned around?*

Aiden shook his head then turned to Luke. *Are you staying?*

Would you like him to?

As many times as the boy signed Luke's name, this was one worry she didn't have. Paul would come around as soon as he heard the whole story, and her mother would adjust, or not.

He looked away but signed, *Always.*

Luke roared with laughter. *Forever.*

At that moment, D'Artagnan stuck his head out to investigate the noise. The horse took one look at Luke, backed his ears, and snorted.

"I'm glad to see you, too, old buddy."

Aiden tugged on his sleeve. *He only likes mom and sometimes me and Buttermilk.*

Luke took a knee. *You and your mom are special. And Buttermilk, too. Do you think D'Artagnan will learn to like me just a little bit?*

The little boy's face screwed up. *Only if you bring him sugar cubes every day.*

It's a promise.

You didn't happen to build an apartment in this mansion for horses. I know it's going to take time for us to rebuild our relationship, and as much as I want to rush to the courthouse today, I want to make sure everyone's happy with us being together."

"Sorry, no." Her laugh lifted a great weight off his shoulders. "I'm sure we can find someplace for you to be."

He stood, drawing Julia in close. "I promise to bring D'Artagnan all the sugar he wants, to love your son as my own, and to wake up beside you for as many mornings as I'm granted."

This was the man she once knew, the one who loved with everything he had.

Life had altered him in ways she was just beginning to understand. She'd accept those changes, the ones on the surface and those at his core. But the man before her was the one she'd once known and planned her life with. A storm sent him reeling into her life only to have deception snatch him away again. A miracle brought him back for good.

"After we get the horses fed and watered, let's head back to the hotel. I've got a wedding to plan."

Luke's eyes widened. "How soon do you want to get married?"

"I was thinking early next year. January is a quiet time for the resort. Don't you think a winter wedding would be beautiful?"

"With you as the bride, how could it not be?"

"Maybe we'll even get some snow."

"I could see you in a fur trimmed gown, and we could leave in a horse drawn sleigh."

The imagery made her heart sing. "As long as you're with me and it isn't sleeting yards of ice that traps us for a week, I'll be happy. After all, you came in on a storm, so it seems fitting we start our lives together with a little weather event."

A word about the author…

Award winning author, Melissa Klein, writes heartwarming romance. She uses southern charm and humor to create everyday heroes who fight extraordinary battles. When away from the laptop, she gardens, creates pottery, and takes care of her loved ones. You can visit Melissa's website at www.melissakleinromance.com.

Thank you for purchasing
this publication of The Wild Rose Press, Inc.

For questions or more information
contact us at
info@thewildrosepress.com.

The Wild Rose Press, Inc.
www.thewildrosepress.com

www.ingramcontent.com/pod-product-compliance
Lightning Source LLC
Chambersburg PA
CBHW070444260626
47161CB00004B/1203

9781509236534